Bets
Up-and-Down Year

Titles in the Polish American Girls Series:

Betsy's
Up-and-Down Year

by Anne Pellowski

Pictures by Wendy Watson

Saint Mary's Press
Christian Brothers Publications
Winona, Minnesota

To the real Betsy
and to all the book Betsys and their
creators because they have brought
so much joy into my life

Genuine recycled paper with 10% post-consumer waste.
Printed with soy-based ink.

The publishing team included Stephan Nagel, development editor and cover designer; Jacqueline M. Captain, copy editor; Alan S. Hanson, production editor; Maurine R. Twait, art director; Kent Linder, graphic designer; pre-press, printing, and binding by the graphics division of Saint Mary's Press.

Republished by Saint Mary's Press, 1998. Originally published by the Putnam Publishing Group. Used with permission.

Printed in the United States of America

Printing: 9 8 7 6 5 4 3 2 1

Year: 2006 05 04 03 02 01 00 99 98

ISBN 0-88489-539-4

Cataloging information
Pellowski, Anne, author. Watson, Wendy, illustrator.
Title: Betsy's Up-and-Down Year
Summary: Betsy's year is filled with growing pains and pleasures. She learns about sibling rivalry, which she thinks explains the bickering among the children in her large and loving Polish Catholic family. Intended for grades 3–5.

1. Polish Americans—Juvenile fiction. 2. Farm life—Juvenile fiction. 3. Wisconsin—Trempealeau County—History—Juvenile fiction. 4. Minnesota—Winona County—History—Juvenile fiction.

Contents

Sibling Rivalry

"What's that you're doing?" Betsy asked her oldest sister.

Linda was sitting in front of the window that separated the dining room from the back porch, every now and then writing frantically in a thick notebook.

"Sssh! I'm observing," she whispered.

"Observing what? And why do we have to whisper?" Betsy wanted to know.

"I'm observing Kristine and Sara and making notes for my Early Childhood Development class. Now get out of here and don't bother me," hissed Linda.

Scattered on the dining-room table were a half-dozen fat textbooks. One of them lay open, and Betsy could see the yellow underlining Linda had made to call attention to certain sentences.

> SIBLING RIVALRY is usually accepted by parents as a natural and almost inevitable condition when there is more than one child in a family. However, even in warm and loving family environments, parents are sometimes shocked at the violent attacks that seem to come out of nowhere.

"It sounds like a disease," Betsy commented. Linda payed no attention to her.

"Is that what you're observing? Sibling rivalry?" Betsy poked her head in front of Linda's so she could see what Kristine and Sara were doing. They were dressing and undressing their dolls, talking softly to them all the while. There didn't seem to be much to observe.

True, Sara looked very different from Kristine, even though they were exactly one year apart. Sara was tall and thin for her seven years, and her light-brown hair hung straight and wispy on either side of her face. Kristine was short and chubby, and her round, perfectly shaped head with its tight white-gold curls made her look as though she belonged in one of the old-fashioned pictures of saints that hung on the walls of Betsy's school. But they certainly didn't look as though they had a disease attacking them.

"What's sibling rivalry?" she asked.

"It's what I'm trying to observe, but you make a better door than a window." Linda's voice was full of exasperation. "I told you to get out of here."

"You didn't say 'Please,'" said Betsy.

"Please, will you leave me alone?" begged Linda.

"I will, but first tell me what sibling rivalry is."

"Siblings are your brothers and sisters, and rivalry is when you're jealous of them, especially the one born after you. That one is your rival because you both try to get your parents' attention at the same time," Linda explained hurriedly and then went back to her observing.

"You mean Sara is my rival?" asked Betsy in astonishment.

Linda nodded her head and kept on writing.

Betsy stared through the window at Sara, trying to see her younger sister in this new light. She did argue with Sara a lot, but not any more than with her other sisters. It was Danny that she quarreled with the most, and he was nine years older than she. Could it be that sibling rivalry skipped around in a family? If so, they must have a lot of it, with ten children.

"How does—" Betsy started to ask for more information, when Linda interrupted her.

"Please! get! away! from! this! window!" The words came out in short, muted barks, accompanied by firm shoves, until Betsy was moved to the middle of the room. She was about to protest when suddenly the front door opened and slammed shut and Julie came tearing through the kitchen into the dining room, her straight brown hair flying.

"Hey, Julie! Did you know I'm your rival?" asked Betsy brightly.

"My what?" Julie stopped in her tracks.

"Your rival. I was born a year after you, so you are probably jealous of me. Are you?"

Before Julie could get over her surprise and answer, the front door opened again and this time Dorothy came in, flushed and sweating from having rushed through her chores.

"Dort, did you know Julie was your rival?" Betsy wanted to share her new knowledge with every member of the family.

"What are you talking about?" asked Dorothy.

"Well, I'm Julie's rival, she's your rival, you're Mona's rival, Mona is Carol's, Carol is Danny's, Danny is Kathy's and Kathy is Linda's. You know—sibling rivalry. It's when brothers and sisters feel jealous of the next one to come along in the family." Betsy felt pretty smart about catching on so fast to something Linda was studying in college. "After all," she thought, "I'm only in third grade. There are probably a lot of kids who wouldn't know how to read those words, and I even know the meaning."

"Come on, tell me, Julie. Are you jealous of me?" Betsy repeated.

Julie eyed her sister warily, as though she suspected some trick behind the question.

"Not any more than you're jealous of Sara," she finally answered.

With a whish and a wham the kitchen door was opened and slammed shut yet again, and Mona came stomping into the room.

"Dorothy, you get right back out there and finish your work. I'm not going to pull down any more hay bales. I've done my share."

"And who pulled down all the bales yesterday? I did, that's who," said Dorothy. She and Mona continued to argue, unable to agree on whose turn it was to feed the rest of the calves. When Danny came in, the two girls turned to him to get his opinion, but he ignored them and went straight to Betsy.

"You left the water running in the pole barn, and now

10

I have to clean up all that wet mess and spread new straw," he scolded her.

"I didn't forget," protested Betsy. "Julie said she'd turn it off."

"I did not," denied Julie. "I told you to stay down there and do it, but you weren't listening."

Just then, Kathy came downstairs, carrying an armload of books. She stared at the dining-room table still strewn with Linda's books and papers.

"There are other people around here who have to study besides you, Linda. I want some space, too, so I can study while I'm making supper." Kathy began to shove Linda's books to one side.

Distracted from her own argument, Betsy glanced at the table and saw the open book, with the sibling-rivalry paragraphs accentuated by the livid yellow streaks of the marker. She could almost read the words from where she was standing.

"Could it be like Pandora's box?" she wondered. She had heard the story about the box that was supposed to stay closed and the inquisitive girl who had to know what was in it; when she had opened the box, all the cares and troubles of the world came flying out. Maybe the words in the open book had caused the attack of fighting.

Quickly, Betsy went to the table and flipped the book shut.

"You lost my place!" shrieked Linda. "I need to refer to those pages while doing my observation."

Betsy jumped with fright at Linda's shriek, but relaxed when she realized there would be no more observing, anyway. Sara had come into the room, crying and holding out a doll's dress that was missing a sleeve.

"Look what Teensie did! She tore my best doll's dress!"

"It was a accident," said Kristine from the doorway. But no one could hear her with all the sobbing, wrangling and quibbling.

Once more the front door opened, and this time it was Mom. "What is going on here? Can't we go off for a Sunday afternoon without finding all of you bickering and quarreling when we come back?"

The children were silent. At last, Dorothy spoke up. "We weren't quarreling."

"Then what was all that noise I heard as I came in?"

"That was an attack of sibling rivalry," said Betsy. At that everyone had to laugh because she used such grown-up words.

"Well, wasn't that it?" Betsy turned to Linda for confirmation. Her sister nodded, still shaking with laughter.

Now the room was noisy again, but this time with giggles and guffaws as Linda explained her assignment and how Betsy had learned about sibling rivalry. Even Sara had forgotten about her crying, because Kathy had assured her it was no problem to sew the sleeve back into the doll's dress.

"I don't believe sibling rivalry is a disease," said Betsy, "but if it is, I'm sure glad it goes away this fast."

She spoke too soon.

The Bottle Lady

Linda went back to her college in Menominee, and Betsy might have forgotten all about sibling rivalry except that one day the following week everything and everybody seemed determined to remind her that it was still there, waiting, like a flu bug, for those moments when the children were most susceptible.

It started with a blizzard during the night. They woke up to find the wind still howling fiercely as it whipped the snow into deep drifts and steep banks.

"No driving to town in this weather," said Dad as he came in from the barn. He called the Farmer's Exchange and then the school, explaining their absences.

"Oh, no! That means I miss my English test! And Sister Gabriel always makes it twice as hard when you have to take it later," cried Mona as she opened the front door and looked desperately at the swirling snow. Disgusted, she slammed it shut and stomped off to her room.

"Are you sure we can't get through?" asked Dorothy, who was aiming at a year of perfect attendance and so far had not missed one day. But once she had stepped outside, even she had to admit that it was hopeless.

Betsy didn't like missing school, either, but secretly she was always glad when a snowstorm kept them home. It felt so cozy and snug in the house, with everyone reading or playing games or working quietly. Often, she didn't even have to do her usual outside chores on such days, because her parents thought it was too dangerous for the younger children to go to the barn and the sheds.

Today Betsy felt especially happy about staying home because on Monday they had stopped at the library and checked out a new batch of books. In second grade she had read most of the Betsy books by Carolyn Haywood, but on Monday, thanks to Dorothy, she had found a new series of books about a different Betsy.

"Take this one," Dorothy had said, holding out a book called *Betsy-Tacy*. "You will just love it, and there are a whole bunch more that follow it."

Betsy had read all the way home, and before she went to bed on Monday night, and again on Tuesday evening. She was more than halfway through the book and couldn't wait to finish it. This morning, as soon as she had eaten breakfast, she settled down in a chair and began the next chapter. It was called "The Sand Store" and was all about bottles of colored sand that Betsy and her friend Tacy sold for pins and pennies.

"My lady bottle!" she cried, remembering an empty syrup bottle in the shape of a lady that was one of her favorite things. Usually Mom bought syrup in gallon pails, but once Betsy had begged Mom to buy one of the lady bottles, and Mom had done so, even though it was more expensive.

"I could put colored sand in her," Betsy thought excitedly. "She can have a blue skirt, a pink blouse, and yellow hair." Putting down her book, she ran to her room and rummaged through the box under her bunk bed until she found the bottle.

"Mom, have you got any sand?" asked Betsy as she came downstairs.

"Sand? It's snowing up a storm and you want sand?" Mom exclaimed in disbelief.

"Just a little," said Betsy. "Enough to fill this bottle."

"There might be some sand in one of the sheds, but I don't think there's any in the house. I'll look this evening at milking time, if you want."

"No, I want it now," said Betsy. She couldn't help allowing a little whine to creep into her voice.

"Well, there's no way to get it now. No one's going out in that storm to look for sand. I'm not even sure there is any."

Betsy stared out at the blowing snow, now piled up as high as the bottom windowpanes on the north side of the house.

"That's what I can put in my bottle! Snow!"

Hastily she put on a coat and threw a scarf around her head. Taking a pail, she opened the door of the back porch, scooped a mound of snow and then stepped back in. Soon she was happily spooning the snow into the bottle.

16

"Mom, where are those coloring drops you use to dye eggs?" asked Betsy, returning to the kitchen.

Mom looked up from the book she was reading. "Good Heavens! First sand and now coloring drops! What on earth are you up to?"

"I want to color some snow in my bottle. That's okay, isn't it? I'm doing it on the back porch."

"I guess it's all right. The food colors are in the cabinet in the pantry. Use only a few drops."

Just as Betsy was backing into the kitchen, hands full of the small bottles, Danny opened the front door. It smacked her in the elbow and sent the three bottles in her right hand flying. One of them had obviously not been capped tightly, because it sprayed a plume of green droplets straight across the linoleum.

"Now look what you've done! Can't you learn to open the door slowly?" yelled Betsy. She felt funny repeating what Mom always said whenever they had such an accidental collision.

"I didn't build these dumb doors the way they are," protested Danny.

"Well, neither did I," said Betsy crossly. "But I'll probably get blamed for spilling the food color." It wasn't fair. Mom was always taking Danny's side, because he was the only boy in the family.

As if she heard Betsy thinking about her, Mom entered the kitchen. She glanced at the tiny green puddles and then spoke. "It's not permanent. Wipe it up quickly with a rag, Betsy."

"Just like I thought," mumbled Betsy. "He causes the mess, but I have to clean it up."

Mom gave her a what's-wrong-now look, so Betsy quickly soaked up the spots of color. Then, picking up the bottle, she saw there was almost no liquid left in it.

"Oh, well," she thought. "I only wanted blue, pink and yellow anyway."

When she returned to the porch, Betsy noticed that the snow had settled down in the bottle, so she had to spoon more in before the line reached the lady's waist. Cautiously, she squeezed a drop of blue coloring into the bottle. It splattered on the snow and against the glass sides, but instead of spreading down into the snow, and making it seem as though the lady had a skirt of blue, the color stayed at the top in a big blotch. It wasn't working out at all the way she had planned. Then she remembered something from the chapter in *Betsy-Tacy*.

"They used colored water over the sand. Maybe if I do the same it will spread through the snow." But when she tried pouring some blue-colored water into the lady bottle, the snow inside melted completely and all she had left was blue liquid up to the waist.

"There's got to be a way of doing this," thought Betsy. "I wish Kathy were here." Kathy was always involved in chemistry experiments and knew a lot about separating liquids and gases and things. But Kathy had stayed at Grandma's house overnight when she heard there was a snowstorm threatening.

"Mona's pretty good in science, too. Maybe she can help me." Betsy ran up the stairs to where Mona lay stretched out on her bed, studying from a thick book.

As soon as Betsy had explained her problem, Mona gave her the answer. "Fill it with snow, then pour in cold colored water up to the waist and set it outside to freeze. As soon as the bottom part is frozen, put in more snow, then the next level of cold water, and let that freeze. Keep on doing it until you get to the top. Only be sure the water is really cold, and pour slowly so you don't melt the level below."

"How simple!" pronounced Betsy. "Why didn't I think of that?"

"'Cause you're not as smart as I am," teased Mona.

Now everything worked perfectly. She put the lady bottle on the outside porch windowsill and went back to reading *Betsy-Tacy*. In an hour, the blue layer was frozen solid.

"It really does look like a skirt!" Betsy was extremely satisfied. She could hardly wait to get the pink blouse part completed. Slowly, with great attention, she spooned in the fresh snow and over it the pink liquid. Then back outside went the bottle, and back to her book went Betsy. It was not until she finished the book that she looked out at her bottle. Instead of being covered by snow as it had been the first time, it was only lightly dusted.

"The storm has stopped," cried Betsy.

"So it has," answered Mom.

Mona came clattering down the stairs.

"The storm is gone. Look, Mom! It's not blowing or snowing one bit. Can't we dig out the cars and get to school after all? I could still make my test. English isn't until sixth period, this afternoon."

"Well, we have to shovel the yard sometime today, but I still don't think you'll get to town because the road hasn't been plowed. Those drifts will be ten feet high."

As if in answer, Dad came in the front door.

"I think we should start digging out. I heard the county snowplow up on the hill. It'll be along any minute, plowing out the road."

"You see! I know we can make it, if we try," cried Mona.

"All right," said Mom, reluctantly putting aside her book. "Everybody outside."

"Oh, Mom, I can't. I'm in the middle of something important," said Betsy. Usually she liked going out with everyone and pitching in to the work of snow removal. Dad attacked the biggest drifts with the plow attached to one of his tractors, but there were many small corners and paths where the tractor couldn't go, and they had to be shoveled out by hand. But this time her bottle lady seemed more urgent.

"We want to stay in, too," said Sara and Kristine, busily engaged with their dolls again.

"Okay," Mom agreed. "You three stay inside. But don't get into trouble and don't touch the stove."

Betsy turned away, offended. Of course she wouldn't touch the stove. Didn't Mom realize that was a warning for babies who didn't know any better?

She returned to the back porch to see if the colored ice inside the lady bottle had melted. No, it was still quite solid. She noticed that the pink blouse extended a bit into the lady's neck.

"I must have poured it in too high," thought Betsy. She spooned in fresh snow, right to the top of the bottle and was just trickling in the yellow water when Kristine appeared at her side.

"Where's the salve?" asked Kristine.

"Why do you want the salve?"

"My doll has a sore and I want to put on salve."

"Salve is for people, not for dolls," said Betsy. "Go away. Don't bother me right now. I have to do this just right." She continued to pour in the yellow water until it was exactly level across the top of the bottle. Slowly and

20

methodically she screwed on the bottle cap and tightened it as best she could.

"There! Now if it tips over, nothing will spill out." Betsy hopped outside again, placed the bottle on the windowsill, and returned to the porch. She was cleaning up the mess she had made when she heard a tremendous crash coming from the direction of the pantry, followed by the sound of Kristine crying. Betsy ran.

"Good grief! What were you doing in there?" asked Betsy as she surveyed the scene. In the pantry was a toppled-over chair and on the floor next to it was Kristine. But the worst part of all was her hair. It was filled with a thick, gooey, yellowy syrup. Glancing up at the shelves, Betsy saw a white plastic bucket, turned on its side, still dripping. The cover of the bucket lay next to Kristine.

"Mom's going to be mad at you," said Betsy. "She was

saving that honey for something special. I heard her say so.''

Kristine had stopped crying, now that she realized she wasn't hurt, and was licking the honey from her cheeks.

"Come on. I'll have to clean up this mess, but first I'll clean you off." Betsy took Kristine by the hand and led her to the bathroom.

"I think you'd better go right into the tub." Betsy ran the water while Kristine stripped off her clothes. "What were you looking for, anyway?" she asked as she rubbed Kristine's honeyed hair with a wet washcloth.

"I told you. The salve. Sara and I are playing doctor and nurse."

"Well, the salve is up there on the high shelf over the tub. Even I can't reach it. Can't you use pretend salve?"

Kristine didn't answer because she had her eyes and mouth screwed up tight to keep out the water and soap from the washcloth Betsy kept sloshing over her head. At last the honey was all washed away. Betsy went to get a clean set of clothes for her sister, while Kristine rubbed herself dry with a towel. In no time at all she was dressed, and once again her hair sprang out in curls around her face, like a golden halo.

"Now I'd better go and clean up the pantry," sighed Betsy. "If Mom saw it, she'd probably say it was my fault, for not watching Kristine." She hadn't yet figured out what explanation she would give for the empty honey pail.

The pantry was a sticky mess. Honey was splattered on most of the cupboards, on the floor and all over the chair that Kristine had brought in from the kitchen. Betsy scrubbed and wiped, rinsing her cloth out every few minutes. She began to get hungry. At last everything was cleaned up, and Betsy lifted the dishpan of dirty water to take it to the kitchen sink.

With a whump! the kitchen door opened, bumped into the pan, and sent it crashing to the floor, splashing sticky honey-water over the linoleum and along the rag rug.

"Oh, no!" cried Betsy.

Dorothy slowly closed the kitchen door and gazed at the sloppy floor.

"Mom sent me to see what time it was," she said in a subdued voice.

Betsy burst into tears.

"I'm sorry, Betsy. I'll come back and help you wipe it up as soon as I tell Mom it's quarter after twelve."

When Dorothy returned, she opened the door very slowly, and as soon as she had taken off her coat and scarf and boots, she went to help Betsy.

"What were you doing in the pantry with a pan of water?" Dorothy asked, more than a little irritated at this extra work.

"You wouldn't believe me if I did tell you," grumbled Betsy.

They had barely finished wiping up the floor and spreading a clean rug, when the snow shovelers returned to the house, cold and hungry.

Mom had begun to take out pots and pans to start dinner when Sara came in, holding out her hands and arms. They were covered with red blotches.

"It pinches, Mom!"

"Mine, too!" piped up Kristine, coming in behind Sara.

Mom looked at their arms with alarm. "What have you been playing with?"

"Salve," answered Sara. "We were playing doctor and nurse and put salve on our dolls, only now it pinches."

"What kind of salve?" asked Mom, already rushing to the playroom where the girls kept their dolls.

Betsy had a horrible suspicion. She hurried to the bathroom and, sure enough, there was a chair standing below the high shelf. She ran to tell Mom and found her staring in disbelief at a round metal container sitting on the playroom floor.

"Dehorning paste! *Święta Maria,*" Mom murmured a prayer in Polish as she always did when she was really worried. Grabbing Kristine and Sara by the arms, she hauled them into the bathroom, meanwhile yelling to Carol, "Call the clinic and ask what the antidote is for dehorning paste. The label says wash with cool water, but find out if there's something we should put on afterward."

In the bathroom, Mom started splashing water madly over Sara's and Kristine's hands and arms. By this time, they were both sobbing so loudly Carol could hardly carry on her phone conversation.

"The doctor says to wash for at least ten minutes in cool water, and then put on some Vaseline. But he says you'd better bring them in after that, just in case."

"Danny, go and start the car," called Mom. "What a blessing we got that snow shoveled away!" She continued to slosh water over the two little girls.

"I'm going with you," announced Mona. "You can drop me off at school on the way to the clinic." She ran upstairs to change.

After ten minutes, Mom brought Kristine and Sara out

of the bathroom. Tenderly she patted the red spots with a soft towel, murmuring, "It's going to be all right." Kristine and Sara whimpered as she smeared Vaseline over the spots, and Mom kept on soothing them with reassurances.

Suddenly, from the back porch came the sound of a soft explosion, as though someone had flung a hard snowball against the window. Betsy ran to make sure her bottle lady was all right, but the moment she glanced at the window she knew something was wrong. There was no sign of the bottle lady.

"She must have fallen," thought Betsy fearfully. "I hope she didn't break."

Yet that was exactly what had happened. The shattered pieces of glass lay in the snow. Betsy blinked back her tears.

"What was that noise I heard? It sounded like a shot," said Mona, coming downstairs, dressed and ready for school.

"My lady bottle," answered Betsy. "It exploded or something."

"Did you fill it right to the top with water and then shut it?" Mona asked, and Betsy nodded.

"Betsy, haven't you ever learned that water expands when it freezes?" said Mona pityingly. "You put too much in and that forced it to break the glass when it froze."

"Well, if you're so smart, why didn't you tell me in the first place?" asked Betsy furiously.

"Come on, Mona, we're leaving," said Mom. Then she turned to Betsy. "I hope you can stay out of mischief this time."

That was too much for Betsy. "Sara and Kristine cause

all the trouble, but I get the scolding," she burst out an-
grily. "And on top of that my lady bottle is broken and
you'll probably never in a million years buy another
one."

"What are you talking about?" asked Mom in bewil-
derment.

"Come on. I'll explain in the car," said Mona.

"Show me your bottle, Betsy," said Carol. "Maybe I
can fix it."

Tearfully, Betsy took her to the back porch and pointed through the window.

"Well, the bottle may be broken, but the lady is whole,
I think," cried Carol. She slipped on a pair of boots and,
without putting on a coat, retrieved the ice lady. Betsy
stared at it in wonder.

"This is neat, Betsy. I couldn't have done it if I tried. Why don't you put her on a pedestal, like a statue? It's so cold out she won't melt as long as she's not in the direct sun."

Betsy gulped. Now that she saw the ice lady up close she thought it was pretty neat, too. It was so smooth and fine it looked as though an artist had carved and polished colored rocks that were pressed together. She and Carol took a stump of wood, propped it up carefully in the snow, and placed the ice lady on it. In the reflected light of the snow, she looked sparkly and special.

When Mom came back from the clinic with Sara and Kristine, Betsy ran out and directed them all to the back of the house, triumphantly showing off her ice masterpiece.

"Maybe I shouldn't give this to you, then," laughed Mom as she dug in a brown grocery bag and pulled out a bottle of syrup in the same lady shape.

"Oh, yes, you should," grinned Betsy as she snatched the bottle.

After they were in the house and had taken off coats, scarves, and mittens, Betsy noticed Kristine's and Sara's arms. The red blotches looked sore and painful. Kristine even had a few on her face, where she had accidentally rubbed her hands before they were washed off.

Betsy felt sorry for them, but at the same time she was annoyed because they were getting all the attention. And they got even more of it a moment later when it was discovered that their dolls had suffered almost worse than they had. The smooth pearly-pink faces and limbs were covered with spots that had blistered and peeled wherever the dehorning paste had touched them. Those beautiful dolls, brand-new at Christmas, now looked as though they were suffering from a terrible disease and couldn't possibly live much longer.

Kristine and Sara were too shocked to cry. Sadly, they cradled their dolls as though they were holding dying babies. Everyone spoke to them softly and tenderly.

Betsy, too, consoled them as best she could, but deep down inside she found herself saying, "It serves you right. That's what you get for not listening to me." She tried to suppress such mean, selfish thoughts, but they kept popping up again until, in a flash, she realized something.

"This is what it meant in Linda's book." Now she could make sense of the idea that sometimes sibling rivalry struck violently, and for no good reason. "The thing is, you probably have to strike back at it."

"I'll give you my doll, the one I got last year for Christmas," Betsy told Sara, and immediately she felt better.

Do-Si-Do
and Away She Goes

"We'd better call for an appointment to get our butchering done. Mary and Ed are coming in a few weeks to pick up their meat," Mom informed Dad one day in mid-February.

Betsy tried not to listen as Mom and Dad discussed which pigs and steers would be slaughtered. The butcher used to do the slaughtering right on the farm, but now, to Betsy's relief, he preferred to do it at his plant in Winona. The roasts, steaks, ribs, hamburger rolls, bones and innards would stay in town at the meat locker to be quick-frozen, but the hams, flank strips and ground meat

Dad would bring home right away.

Betsy looked forward to the making of the hams, dried beef and sausage, especially the days when they were being smoked. She never complained about having to carry extra armloads of hickory wood to keep the fire under the meats burning slowly, because it gave her a chance to sniff deeply the smoky, meaty smell that swirled out of the smokehouse during the few moments the door was opened.

"Measure out four cups of salt for me," Mom told Betsy when the day had arrived. After the brine was ready, the meat to be smoked was put in to soak awhile. Mom then turned to the big washtub of ground meat. She poured in a jar of mustard seed and sprinkled a lot of ground pepper and salt over the meat.

"I'll help you mix it in," offered Betsy. It felt good to thrust her hands deep into the meat and squish it around until the seasonings were spread all through.

Mom brought out the sausage-stuffing machine and put a casing over the exit hole, and while Betsy fed the meat into the machine, Danny turned the handle. The casing in Mom's hand filled up until it was taut and plump and round. Dad tied off each end, then tied the ends together and slipped the sausage onto a pole stretched between two chairs, so that it could dry off.

"Get on there, you *wurst!*" said Dad to one fat sausage that kept slipping and sliding under his fingers, refusing to stay in place long enough to let him tip the string over the pole.

"That's a *kielbasa,*" said Mom with a laugh.

"Well, I call it a *wurst,*" answered Dad, annoyed at both Mom and the sausage.

"Does it matter what you call it as long as it tastes good?" asked Kathy, trying to end the dispute. Betsy agreed with her. She didn't like her parents to argue.

As they went out to hang up the sausages in the smokehouse, Betsy felt a drop of water land on her nose. She looked up and realized that all of the icicles on the sunny side of the house were slowly dripping.

"My ice lady!" she cried, running to the other side of the house. Picking it up, she saw that a tiny trickle of blue water lay on the stump.

"She's melting! What am I going to do?" She couldn't bear the thought of her lovely ice lady melting and disappearing. She ran to Mom.

"My ice lady's melting! I want to put her in the freezer until it gets cold again," she said.

"But we're about to put in our fresh supply of meat," said Mom.

"By the time it's ready to bring home, maybe the weather will be cold again," said Betsy.

"I don't know about that," said Mom. "I think you should let her stay outside until she melts."

"Please, Mom. I promise I'll take her out when you bring home the meat."

"All right, but remember, a promise is a promise."

For the next two weeks, the nights were crisp and cold, but the days were warm enough so that the icicles were always dripping.

On the first Friday in March they made ready the space in Danny's room where their cousins usually slept. Aunt Mary and Uncle Ed stayed in town with Grandma and Grandpa, but Mike, Dave and John came to the farm. Saturday passed in a frenzy of games and chores

31

and eating and more games. On Sunday Grandma invited everyone to dinner, and there was more good eating. Afterward, they all played cards, but soon the children got restless.

"Let's do some square dancing," suggested Kathy. "We have enough persons for eight couples." She danced every week with a group, and was always begging her parents and Danny to go with her, but they never would.

"I'm sorry, Kathy, but my dancing days are over," lamented Grandma. "My feet can't take it anymore."

"Then you can sit and watch," said Kathy, "and Grandpa can play the tunes on his harmonica. Let me see, now: Kris, you be partner with Julie; Sara, you're with John; Betsy, you take Dave; Dorothy and Mike, you stand over there; Mona, you're good with Danny here; Mom and Dad, stand in the middle there; Aunt Mary and Uncle Ed, go next to Betsy; that leaves you for my partner, Carol." Before they knew what had happened, Kathy had paired everyone up and placed them in a circle.

"Don't you know I've got two left feet?" protested Uncle Ed, but Kathy paid no attention to him.

"Hmm," she said, looking around the kitchen. "This isn't quite enough room. Grandma, it's all right if we move the table and chairs to the back porch, isn't it?" Since she was already carrying out a chair when she asked, there wasn't much Grandma could do except say "Yes."

Now the kitchen seemed spacious. Again Kathy lined up the partners in a circle.

"First I have to teach you some basic steps," she said. "We'll start with Honor Your Partner, Promenade, Circle Right and Left, and Do-Si-Do."

"Do. See Do. See Do Dance," said Mike, pointing to his partner, Dorothy. Everyone groaned and laughed, and then Kathy began the demonstration.

Honor Your Partner was easy because that was only bowing. Promenade was a walking step and not too hard, either. For Circle Right and Left, dancers simply joined hands and walked in a circle, in the direction Kathy called out. But with Do-Si-Do the steps began to get a little difficult because each person had to circle around his or her partner back to back, first touching right shoulders and then left. Betsy kept forgetting and always started off wrong way around. But Kathy wouldn't go on to the next steps until they had the first four down pat.

"Now you're going to learn how to Swing, Balance, do a Grand Right and Left and an Allemande Right and Left."

"What about Allewoman Right and Left?" asked Uncle Ed. He was always making puns, most of which Betsy didn't understand, but at this one she laughed.

The four new steps were much more complicated. Each dancer had to hold on to his or her partner in just the right way and then grab for the right hand or the left hand of the next person. At times they were supposed to weave in and out and meet up with their partners again, but invariably the circle ended in a tangle of hands and arms.

Again and again Kathy took them through the new steps, occasionally inserting one from the first four they had learned. Finally she was satisfied they could do them all pretty well.

"There are at least four more steps, but I think that's enough for the first time. Now we'll try a dance. Are you ready, Grandpa?"

He played a lively song, and Kathy called out the instructions. They made it halfway through the dance before it collapsed in confusion.

"Once more," said Kathy. "Try harder this time."

Grandpa played and Kathy called, and everyone danced with great concentration, but they still did not make it to the end.

"It must be because we need more room," Kathy excused them. "Let's try it once more."

"After this round we have to get going," insisted Aunt Mary.

Kathy quickly reviewed the Allemande, and the dancers took their starting positions.

> Honor your partner, don't be late;
> Swing her like you'd swing on a gate!
> Then Promenade.

Betsy kept her eyes focused upward and avoided looking at her feet. She saw Kathy's long blond hair go rippling past; then Aunt Mary's deep-honey-colored hair fanned out, lifted and fell in a soft swirl. It was almost as distracting as looking down, because it made Betsy think about shampoo commercials on television instead of dance steps.

Circle right and make it grand . . .

"Clockwise! I must go clockwise," Betsy reminded herself. First John's right hand, wiry and small like hers; then Uncle Ed's left hand, with its neatly cut, buffed nails; then Mike's right hand, with the nails bitten off; and Dad's left hand, rough and grainy from all the farm work and so big it swallowed up her own. In and out Betsy wove, and so did the other dancers.

Now change it to an Allemande!

Betsy relaxed and let herself be led by the music and the hands of the other dancers.

Find your partner and then you know
Make a little Do-Si-Do!

They kept circling in the Allemande, and when Betsy met up with Dave again they do-si-doed to each other.

Balance with your partner just so;
Now give her a swing and away she goes!

Everyone took two steps back and two forward for the Balance, and then Dave swung Betsy as hard as he could. As she whirled, she could see the other dancers twirling in their spaces. It made her dizzy, but at the same time it was so exhilarating she wanted it to go on and on. The feeling of having completed the dance without a mistake was so satisfying, the couples could hardly bring themselves to stop.

"You see, I told you it was easy to catch on with a little practice," said Kathy to Mom and Dad. "Why don't you come with me this Wednesday?"

"Maybe we will at that," said Mom.

"You're going dancing in Lent?" Grandpa looked shocked.

"I go every Wednesday," said Kathy.

"Well, I don't think it's right, dancing in Lent." Grandpa shook his head.

"But, Grandpa, Lent has already started and you didn't say anything about dancing today," objected Betsy. How could something as thrilling as what she had just experienced be wrong?

"Sunday is Sunday, not Lent," said Grandpa.

Kathy was about to say something more when Mom signaled to her with her eyes.

"I won't go if it upsets you, Grandpa. I have a lot of chemistry experiments anyway, so it won't hurt to give up dancing for Lent," said Kathy.

Betsy knew about giving up things for Lent. She tried hard not to eat candy, and saved up for special offerings to help the poor. But that was different from dancing.

"It can't be wrong to do something that makes you feel so free," she thought. Before she had time to ponder it further, Mom changed the subject, from dancing to meat, because Aunt Mary and Uncle Ed were getting ready to leave.

"Roman will take the pickup and follow you to the locker, Ed. Your meat and ours is already separated.

Carol, you and Mona go with him to help load up."

After goodbyes were exchanged, they hurried to the pickup and the two cars parked in front.

"Are they bringing our meat home today?" asked Betsy.

"Mm-hmm. All of it," said Mom.

"Does that mean I have to take my ice lady out of the freezer?"

"Yes. We'll need every inch of space."

"Can't I leave it in a corner? It doesn't take up much room."

"Betsy, you promised!" Mom reminded her. "She's very pretty, but she has to go. We're almost finished with the new bottle of syrup. You can make another ice lady, and if she melts, you can always empty the bottle and start over. Only this time remember to leave space at the top for the ice to expand."

"As if I'd ever make that mistake again!" thought Betsy.

As soon as they got home, she took her ice statue outside and contemplated it fondly. She couldn't bear to watch it melt, the way their snowmen and snowwomen did, getting more shapeless each day until they were finally nothing but dirty lumps of snow.

"I'll take it out to the animal cemetery," she decided. After carrying it to the corner of the apple orchard where they buried their pets and other small animals, she propped it on a stump and placed some evergreen branches all around. It looked like a statue in church, gazing serenely over the congregation.

"Goodbye, ice lady," whispered Betsy. "Do-Si-Do and away you go," she added, but she did not feel like dancing now.

Sewing Spree

Betsy didn't make any more ice ladies that winter, partly because the weather was too warm, but mostly because she wanted to leave intact the memory of her first lovely lady of yellow, pink and blue. She didn't have many tiffs with her siblings, either.

"I wonder if it's because we're all trying hard to be extra good during Lent," she thought one evening as the family said their special prayers at the supper table.

Afterward she thought about it some more as Kathy helped her with a problem she was having in making two seams meet. Kathy had taught her how to sew, and now Betsy was working on her first piece, with brand-new material that Mom had given her. When it was finished, it would be a wraparound skirt to wear with a blouse she had at gotten at Christmas.

As Kathy patiently undid the seams and once more showed her how to get them right, Betsy decided she had not given in to jealousy or rivalry because she had been too busy to even think about such things. And Kathy was so cheerful, always ready to guide her without taking over the project.

"When you get that belt on correctly, you'll be almost finished," Kathy said encouragingly. "You should easily have it ready by Easter."

She was right, because on Easter Sunday Betsy wore her new skirt, feeling immensely pleased with herself and the world. The weather was so pleasantly warm that April day, she went to church wearing only a heavy cardigan sweater over the blouse and skirt.

Easter Monday was just the opposite: cold and rainy. Mom drove with Betsy to town to meet her cousin Rob at the train depot. By the time the train pulled in, it was raining so hard they could not see out of the car windows. Mom had to keep the car at a creeping pace all the way home.

Once there, she went with Danny and Mona out to the barn to help Dad set up the new manure loader.

"You stay in the house," she ordered the younger children. "I don't want you pestering us."

"This is the pits," said Rob as he stood next to Betsy on the back porch, staring out at the rain. "I wanted to go outside."

"It sure is," agreed Betsy. She searched around for something that would bring back the good feelings of Easter Sunday. "Want to play a game?"

"No," said Rob irritably.

"I think I'll start to sew something," she said at last, moving to the corner of the dining room where the sewing machine stood. There were pieces of mint-green cloth draped over the open cover, and on top of the cloth was a thin booklet and pattern pieces.

"Guess I can't. Kathy has her stuff here," said Betsy.

"You really know how to sew?" asked Rob.

"Sure," answered Betsy. On the floor she spotted a narrow strip of green cloth that Kathy had cut away from her pattern. Picking it up, she tucked it under the needle, pressed the knee pedal, and sewed a straight line down the edge of the strip.

"Neat," said Rob, leaning over the machine. "But what are all those dials and numbers for?"

"Those are for fancy stitches. Kathy knows how to do them, but I don't."

Rob bent over the booklet. "Look! Here it shows you how to make them."

Betsy peered at the pages Rob was holding open and looked at the diagrams as he read aloud.

"'Set Red Lever at 3. All settings on left of plate are controlled by the outer knob. All settings on right of plate are controlled by the inner knob.' This sounds easy. Let's try making Design M—the one that looks like a spinning top."

Betsy was about to object, but Rob was already reading the complete instructions and carrying them out.

"'Lift needle from fabric. Pull inner knob and move selector to Position M. Lower needle and foot and proceed.'"

The machine whirred, but instead of sewing in a straight line, the needle moved from side to side, first in narrow stitches, then wider ones, then narrower ones again, making a line of designs that looked like tops spinning one below the other.

"It works!" cried Rob.

"They look just like the ones in the book!" exclaimed Betsy. She couldn't believe he had done it that simply, especially since it had taken her so long to master sewing in a straight line.

"Let's make all the designs," said Rob. "Only we need a bigger cloth. This scrap is almost covered already."

"I'll get one," said Betsy. She ran to the hamper in the playroom where Mom kept odd scraps that they were allowed to use in playing with their dolls. After scrabbling around a bit she located a square of white cotton cloth that was still fairly clean and unwrinkled.

"The stitches will show up nicely on this," she thought.

Back at the machine, Rob was about to move Kathy's mint-green cloth and patterns to the table.

"Don't," warned Betsy. "She'll be mad if she comes home from work and sees we moved her stuff. Leave it on the machine. We'll fold it over to get it out of the way."

"I'll do a row and then you try it," said Rob. He placed the white square under the needle, adjusted the knobs, lowered the foot and pressed the pedal. Out came another row of designs, only this time they looked like pale spring beech leaves lined up on snow.

"Now it's my turn," said Betsy. The stitch she selected made a row of tiny peaks that looked like a lineup of mountains seen from far away.

Back and forth they alternated, making zigzags and curves and even stitches that looked like castle tops.

"Something's wrong," said Rob. "The stitches aren't holding."

Betsy stared at the last row Rob had attempted. The thread looked loose and out of line. A shudder of guilt passed through her. What if they had wrecked the machine?

"I'm sure I followed the directions," said Rob.

"Let's quit," said Betsy, stretching forward to see the clock in the kitchen. A glimpse told her Kathy was due home any moment. She heard a car drive into the yard and, with a sinking feeling, listened for the front door.

"Where is everybody?" Kathy called from the kitchen.

Neither Betsy nor Rob answered.

Kathy came to the dining-room door and took in everything with one swift glance.

"What are you up to? Did you muss up my sewing?"

Still Rob and Betsy said not a word. Kathy approached them like an angel of doom.

"My thread! You've used up almost all my thread," she said, in disbelief.

Betsy looked at the machine. The empty spool was showing through; there was only half of a layer of thread left. She had not even thought of that problem because of her fear that the machine was broken.

"And I suppose the bobbin is empty, too," said Kathy as she lifted away their cloth, slid aside the metal plate, and took out the bobbin. There was not a whisper of thread left in it.

That made Kathy more upset but relieved Betsy. Now she was sure they had not broken the machine. With no thread in the bobbin the upper thread had nothing to latch onto and became slack. If it was only a matter of thread, she would offer to buy more. She was about to say so, but Rob beat her to it.

"I brought some spending money. I'll buy you more thread," he said.

"But I wanted to sew tonight, and I have no more spools of this color."

Betsy and Rob knew it was highly unlikely anyone would drive to town just to buy two small spools of thread. Betsy was going to say she was sorry when she saw a look of alarm settle on Kathy's face.

"My neck facing!" she wailed. "What have you done with it?" She picked up the scrap of mint-green cloth they had first used for their practice stitches.

"It was on the floor," explained Betsy. "I thought it was a scrap you were throwing away."

"Well, it's not! I needed it to face the V neck opening on my dress, and I don't have any material left. I used every bit of it, and it took me ages to lay out the pattern so I could get all the parts on without piecing them."

Kathy was so overcome by the thought it had all been for nothing, she burst into tears.

Mom came in to find her still sobbing. Silently she listened to Kathy's tale of woe and looked at the facing.

"It's not such a tragedy," she said. "Give me the number of that thread color and I'll call the sewing store to see if it's in stock. Then I'll call Roman and he can pick it up on his way home from work."

"And what am I supposed to do about the facing? I never get it right if I have to piece it." Kathy was a little mollified but not enough to stop her tears completely.

"Betsy and Rob will have to snip out the stitches they made. They can use a tiny manicure scissors."

"Yes, we'll do it," Betsy and Rob agreed eagerly.

"And cut a hole in it," complained Kathy. "No, thanks, I'll do it myself." She went in search of some Kleenex and a pair of manicure scissors.

"I'm sorry, Kathy," Betsy apologized when her sister returned.

"All right, you're sorry. But stay away from my sewing in the future." Kathy grudgingly accepted the apology and began the tedious task of snipping out the tiny stitches.

Betsy felt terrible, and she could see Rob was uncomfortable, too. Even when Mom looked at the square lined with the pretty stitches of mint green and complimented them on their handiwork, Betsy was left with a tight, sad feeling in her middle. Kathy was the last person she wanted to hurt.

"I said I was sorry," Betsy told herself. "And I offered to pick out the stitches. What more could I do?" She defended herself with every reason she could think of, but somehow she still did not feel right.

44

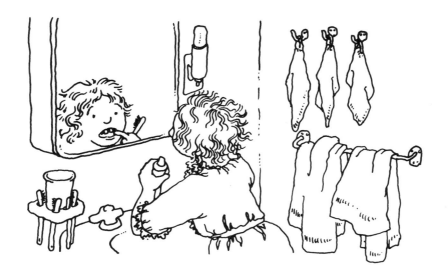

Clogs and Spaces

The vague, unhappy feeling stayed with Betsy for weeks. Kathy seemed friendly enough, now that her dress was finished and had turned out well. Still, Betsy had the sensation of something not quite right every time she looked into her eyes in the mirror.

To make matters worse, she began to notice more and more the space between her front teeth. Every morning and evening, before and after brushing her teeth, she examined it carefully.

"I'm sure it's getting wider," she said to herself. The space had never bothered her before, but now it seemed to give her a funny, divided look when she smiled with her mouth open.

"I'll just have to remember to smile with my lips shut," she told herself.

There was another thing about herself that didn't look right, she decided, and that was her feet, or rather, what was on them. Her plain brown lace-up shoes seemed very old-fashioned. What she wanted more than anything in the world was clogs. All the girls in her class either had a pair or were getting one soon, but Mom wouldn't let her buy any.

"Why can't I have clogs?" she asked plaintively.

"Because they're too expensive, and you know we only buy you shoes once a year, just before school starts. The ones you have must last until then," said Mom firmly.

"If you get me a pair of clogs now, I won't ask for another pair of shoes in August. Honest, I won't."

"No! If I buy them for you, all the others will want a pair, too. I don't want everyone clump-clumping around this house in clogs. Besides, they're ugly."

"They are not," protested Betsy. "If they're so ugly, why are all the girls wearing them?"

"That's the mystery to me," said Mom. "What some people will wear just to keep in style is beyond me. Clogs will probably be out of fashion before the summer is over."

"They will not!" Betsy disputed heatedly. "People have been wearing clogs for hundreds of years. And in Japan and Holland *everybody* wears them." Betsy got a lot of postcards from her Aunt Anne and Aunt Millie when they traveled to foreign countries, and she felt on sure ground because she had pictures to prove her point.

"This isn't Japan and it isn't Holland." Mom was beginning to get exasperated. "Furthermore, I believe they don't wear them so much anymore in those places. You can't convince me they're comfortable."

"How do you know?" asked Betsy boldly. "Did you ever try on a pair?"

"I don't have to. I just know they're uncomfortable."

"Shoes are different from food, I suppose," countered Betsy. "You're always telling us we won't know if we like it unless we try some. Well, I'd like to try a pair of clogs."

"You *would* sneak in an argument like that," laughed Mom. "All the same, you are not getting a pair of clogs, and that's final."

Betsy sighed. Now she wished she had not argued so much. Sometimes if she approached her mother little by little, she could get her to see how important it was to do or to have certain things. But once Mom had made up her mind like that, it was impossible to sway her.

The next day one of the girls in her class came to school wearing a brand-new pair of clogs—the expensive kind.

"It's not fair that some kids get to have the best of everything," thought Betsy. She knew it was wrong to be so envious, but the feeling expanded inside her like the ice that had burst her lady bottle.

At recess, the children went to the playground and the sound of at least a dozen pairs of clogs on the hard cement was full and satisfying, at least to Betsy's ears.

"They don't go clomp-clomp," she thought. "It's more like thonk, thonk." Her own shoes made no sounds at all as she skipped and hopped and ran.

All afternoon Betsy daydreamed about clogs. Twice Miss Brandt called on her, and she couldn't find the place on the page they were reading. During library period, she sat with a book in front of her but never turned a page. Instead of seeing the words, she was seeing a whole new wardrobe of clogs and all the best kinds of clothes. They were lined up as neatly as the edges of the book pages, and they were all her size. When the dismissal bell rang, Betsy didn't move from her seat. She was still gazing off into the distance.

"Betsy, are you spaced out or something?" asked Christie.

Betsy turned to her friend and laughed with her mouth wide open. It was the worst moment for her to forget to close her lips, because Jimmy was standing right behind Christie, and he never let an opportunity to tease go by.

"Yeah, she's spaced out all right. Like Bugs Bunny." Jimmy put his thumb behind his two front teeth and stuttered, "Uh! Uh! Uh! What's up, Doc?"

Betsy snapped her mouth shut, turned around to her desk and began gathering her books.

"I am not going to cry. I am not going to cry," she repeated to herself over and over, but she could feel the first tears spilling out.

"Oh, Betsy, I'm sorry. I didn't mean it that way," apologized Christie as she gave Jimmy a withering look.

Betsy couldn't bring herself to turn around and tell Christie it was all right, because it wasn't. Jimmy was the worst teaser in the class, and once he started on someone he kept it up for weeks. She fled out of the room and down the stairs, turned right toward Cotter High School, and ran the long block to the lot where Danny always parked the car. He was already inside, waiting for everyone to get out of school.

"What's the matter with you?" asked Danny, seeing Betsy's tears.

Betsy didn't answer.

"What's the matter?" Carol came bouncing up with her arms full of books.

"Nothing," muttered Betsy. She thrust her head into the corner and continued to cry softly.

"What's the matter?" repeated Mona and Dorothy and Julie and Sara as, one by one, they came to the car.

"She's got a bad case of nothing," said Danny as he started up the car and smoothly eased it out of the parking spot and into the street.

"Mind your own business!" bawled Betsy. She didn't want them to know what Jimmy had said, but at the same time she did want them to realize that she had had a mortal blow to her self-esteem. She felt they should be sympathetically silent.

"Did you get hurt somewhere?" asked Carol.

Betsy shook her head and grunted.

"Did Miss Brandt scold you?" asked Mona.

Again Betsy shook her head.

"I'll bet someone was teasing her," said Julie.

Betsy sat in her corner, quiet and tense, and made no move or noise to deny it. "They'd better not ask what the teasing was about, because I'm not telling," she thought.

But her sisters asked no more questions, and Danny was too busy driving to say anything more.

At home, Betsy tried to scoot past her mother and escape to her room, but Mom noticed right away that something was wrong. She took Betsy by the arm and led her to the back bedroom.

"Come on. Tell me all about it." Mom sat on the bed and took Betsy in her lap.

Betsy leaned her face against Mom's chest and let the tears flow. A tiny, inner voice tried to tell her that sitting on a lap was much too babyish for a third-grader who was about to pass into fourth grade, but it was stilled by the warm solace of her mother's arms and the reassurance that no one else was looking. When the heaviest tears had been shed, Betsy told Mom about Jimmy's taunting.

"He called me Bugs Bunny and he went like this." Betsy shoved her thumb into her mouth and demonstrated.

"Don't you want to be my funny little bunny?" teased Mom gently, and Betsy had to giggle a bit.

"Isn't there some way I can move my teeth closer together, and not have them stick out so much?" she asked.

"You're due for a checkup at the dentist anyway, so I'll make an appointment with Dr. Madden as soon as I can. But I don't want you moping around until then. If Jimmy starts teasing you, just wiggle your nose and smile as wide as you can and say, 'Don't look too far into the hole, Doc, or it may swallow you up.'"

Betsy snickered and then sighed. Mothers were very comforting and they often gave good advice, but sometimes they didn't know what life was really like in third grade. There were only two weeks of school left, thank goodness, and for that amount of time she would try to steer clear of Jimmy. Maybe Dr. Madden would suggest something she could do over the summer so she would start fourth grade with nice, even teeth.

"Okay now?" asked Mom, giving Betsy a hug.

Betsy nodded.

"I want you to go with Kathy for a walk along the line fence. The cows seem to be getting through somewhere. I'll see that Julie does your chores."

A few minutes later, after she had changed into old clothes, Betsy was following Kathy up the road and across the fields. Kathy was so silent, Betsy thought she might still be angry about the sewing. She caught up with her sister and smiled at her tentatively. Kathy returned the smile, still not saying a word, as though they shared a secret.

"She's not mad," thought Betsy with relief.

The oats field they were passing flowed out like a tufted, thick green bathmat that was too pretty to step on, while the cornfield spread out over the low hill ahead like a brown quilt with rows of green yarn ties. Along the edge of the fields stretched a barbed-wire fence, holding back the leafy tangles and thickets of the underbrush and woods. It was soothing to tramp along in the May sunshine, hardly making a sound.

They came upon a thick cluster of mayflowers and Betsy called out, "Wait! I want to pick some." She started to snap off the flowers with the longest stems. Kathy stooped down next to her and also began to gather a bunch. When they each had a handful, they continued walking along the fence, checking it carefully for loose wires and sagging posts.

Suddenly, through a space in the brambles, Betsy spied a round hollow under a tall tree, filled with yellow splotches that trembled and nodded.

"Could those be butterflies?" she asked.

Soundlessly, Kathy lifted up the barbed wire and they crept up to the hollow. Betsy tripped and fell against a dead bush, sending crackles of noise in every direction, but no wings were lifted in fright.

"It's a patch of violets," she cried. "Only they're yellow. I've never seen yellow violets before. They look more like pansies."

A light breeze rippled over the flowers, lifting their petals so that they almost seemed to open and close like butterfly wings. With her eyes shining as brightly as the violet centers, Betsy looked up at Kathy, eager to check whether she could feel the same magical atmosphere.

"Places like this almost make me believe in fairies," said Kathy softly.

Betsy had been thinking exactly the same thought.

The two girls sat there for a long time, dreaming of happy spirits. When they left they didn't pick any of the violets; it was better to leave them, hidden away in the brushy woods.

The Buffalo Farm

"Did you make my dentist appointment?" Betsy asked Mom a few days before school ended.

"Yes, I did, for next Monday," said Mom. "But I'm thinking we'd better change it."

"Why?"

"I forgot all about that auction I want to go to. They're selling a hay rake, and we need one bad."

"Can't Linda take me?"

"She has tests, and Kathy starts her summer job Monday. I think we should postpone the appointment."

"What about Grandma?" Betsy was persistent because she wanted to hear what Dr. Madden had to say as soon as possible.

"I hate to keep bothering her."

"She'll do it, I know she will. Let me call her."

"All right," Mother agreed reluctantly.

"Sure, I'll be glad to take you," said Grandma as soon as Betsy had asked her the favor. "Why don't you come after church on Sunday and stay over?"

"Thanks, Grandma. I'll see you then."

Friday was Memorial Day, and the weather was cool and rainy.

"No picnic today," said Dad as he came in from morning chores.

"Let's have a picnic right here in the house," said Dorothy.

"Okay," said Mom. "I wasn't intending to do any cooking, anyway."

Kathy made a cake and Linda made potato salad. When noontime came, Carol heated up the wieners and made a platter of hot dogs.

"This is what I like best about picnics," said Betsy, holding up her paper plate. "No dishes to wash."

"I'm going to sit under the trees," said Dorothy, heading for the back porch.

Betsy saw it was a pretend game, so she joined in. "I want some shade, too." She found a spot under the big table next to Dorothy and Julie. Soon Sara and Kristine got the idea and sat down at the end of the row.

"Watch out for ants," said Dorothy.

"Oh! I think one just bit me on the leg," said Betsy, slapping at her calf. "Look! There's one on your arm." She pointed to Julie.

"He can go up into my armpit for all I care!" Julie was too busy eating to be bothered by imaginary ants.

The other girls giggled so much at her answer they

could hardly continue their picnic lunch. Kristine, who had her knees pulled up in front of her legs with her paper plate resting on them, swayed from side to side so far that an olive rolled off her plate.

Suddenly she lifted up her plate, straightened out her legs and said, "Now one is crawling in my crack!"

Betsy almost choked on a mouthful of hot dog, but she managed to squeak out her question: "Your crack?"

"In the crack behind my knee," explained Kristine.

"Her crack!" hooted and shrieked the other girls, finding it so funny they could not eat.

"What on earth is all this commotion about?" asked Mom, coming out onto the porch.

"Teensie said an ant is crawling in her—" Betsy was laughing too hard to finish the sentence.

"Are there ants on the porch?" asked Mom. "I'll have to put out some ant traps."

The girls found this funnier than ever and screamed with laughter.

"An ant trap—for the ant—in Kristine's crack," gasped Dorothy, pointing to her sister's leg.

"You crazy kids!" Mom shook her head and left the porch.

The girls kept up their pretend game for the entire afternoon, and if the laughing stopped all someone had to do was ask, "Kristine, is the ant still in your crack?" and that set them off again.

When Saturday turned out to be as rainy and cold as Friday they continued their game and even convinced Mom to let them have another picnic lunch under the back-porch table.

Sunday was a beautiful day, and after church Dad dropped Betsy off at Grandma's house. It seemed too quiet there after the noisy fun of her home for the past two days. She wished she had asked Mom if one of her sisters could stay overnight with her.

"I'd like to take a drive out to Pine Creek cemetery this afternoon," said Grandma.

"Fine by me," said Grandpa.

Now Betsy wished more than ever that one of her sisters was with her.

"Do you want to sit up in front with us?" asked Grandma as they were about to get into the car.

"I'd rather sit in back," said Betsy. She didn't have any of her sisters for company, so at least she intended to enjoy the luxury of having the whole seat to herself. "I can look out of both windows," she said happily.

When they were more than halfway to Pine Creek, Betsy saw a field with huge brown animals grazing in it.

"The buffalo farm!" she cried. She had passed that way a number of times with Mom.

"Yes, that's Vic's place," said Grandpa.

"Vic who?" asked Betsy.

"My cousin Victor," said Grandpa.

"And my classmate," said Grandma with a laugh. "The mischief he used to get into with my brothers!"

"Can't we stop?" asked Betsy.

"Not now," said Grandma. "I want to get to the cemetery. If there's time, we'll stop on the way back."

The cemetery was at the top of a steep hill overlooking Pine Creek. Betsy helped Grandma and Grandpa pull all the weeds from their family plot, and then she went to the pump several times for pails of water so Grandma could water the plants she had brought. It was peaceful working there in the bright sunshine, accompanied by the soft sounds of the wind brushing against the two rows of tall pine trees. By the time they had finished, the gravesite looked neat and pretty, with its outline of pansies and petunias.

After one last silent prayer, Grandma and Grandpa were ready to go.

"There's still time to stop at the buffalo farm, isn't there?" asked Betsy.

"It has been some time since we had a visit with Victor," said Grandma. Grandpa nodded his head and Betsy knew it was settled: they would stop.

Vic greeted them in Polish, and Betsy answered as her grandparents had taught her: *"Na wieki wieków, amen."*

"Who is this?" asked Vic in English.

"One of Angeline's girls," answered Grandma. They went back to speaking in Polish.

"I'm going to look at the buffalo," said Betsy.

"Don't climb over the fence," said Vic.

The buffalo had come in from the big field and were standing by the long feeding troughs near an open shed. The huge bulls lifted their shaggy heads as Betsy came near the slatted wood fence and peered through one of the narrow spaces. The buffalo were so big she could see only part of them.

"He didn't say I couldn't climb *on* the fence," thought Betsy. She placed her right foot in a space between the boards, then her left foot in a higher space, and after one more step up she could see over the fence.

The entire herd was looking at her. Some of the buffalo stared up through their slanted, fierce-looking eyes while others lowered their heads so the horns seemed to be pointing straight at her. Even the buffalo calves looking at her so solemnly seemed big compared to the calves they had on the farm.

Slowly, several of the buffalo moved in her direction. Betsy stayed where she was, wanting to get a good, close look. But when they came to within a few feet of the fence she began to get scared.

"Shoo! Shoo!" she cried, waving one arm at them.

The buffalo stopped and stared at Betsy, and Betsy stared back at them.

Finally, one great bull stepped forward, stretched out his head and gave a deep grunt.

"I'd better get out of here," thought Betsy.

She swung down her right foot and then tried to release her left one, but it was caught tight. The bull took another step, and now his mouth was right next to the space where her left foot remained stuck.

"Help!" cried Betsy, but not too loudly.

The buffalo flicked his long, rough tongue and began to lick Betsy's foot and her hands where they clung to the fence. She let go of the boards and fell backward on the soft grass, her skirt ballooning down over her shoulders and head, her left foot still caught.

"He-blub." She tried to scream, but the cloth of her skirt filled her mouth, so she pushed it away.

The buffalo's scratchy tongue slurped around her ankle.

"Help!" This time she screamed loud enough to bring Grandma and Grandpa and Vic.

"Did you hurt yourself?" asked Grandma, trying to be serious, but unable to hold back her laughter because Betsy looked so silly there, hanging upside down by one leg.

"They can't hurt you. They're just looking for something to eat," said Vic. "It's their suppertime."

Betsy merely looked at him. Who was he trying to fool? She was convinced those monster buffaloes could push down the fence and come stampeding right over her.

Grandpa lifted Betsy up, and Grandma twisted her ankle gently to one side until she could slip the foot out of its trap.

"Goodness! It's starting to swell," said Grandma. "Maybe we'll have to take you to the doctor tomorrow instead of the dentist."

"Oh, no, Grandma, it doesn't hurt at all," said Betsy, which was not the truth, because her ankle felt very sore.

"That's enough buffalo watching for today," said Grandma. "Get in the car and keep your left leg up on the seat. That will hold down the swelling."

When they got home, Grandpa propped Betsy up in an easy chair and put a cold compress on her ankle. She sat there all evening, munching on popcorn and watching television.

"Let me look at your ankle now," said Grandma before Betsy went up to bed. "Hmmm. Pretty good. No more swelling."

With relief, Betsy hopped up the stairs, using her right foot.

The Willow Wind Warbler

"Goodbye, Linda!" said Betsy as she gave her sister a hug. Linda was about to board a plane that would take her to New York. Then she would change planes and fly to Guyana, where Aunt Millie was now living. Aunt Millie worked for the government, and every few years she was sent to a new place. When the family had first learned she was moving to Guyana, everyone had asked, "Where is that?" So they had checked in the encyclopedia and learned all about the small country on the northeast coast of South America.

"Don't get lost in the wild mountains," said Betsy. Since she had read that much of Guyana was covered with thick forests and wild mountains, she wasn't sure it

61

was a safe place for Linda to go.

"I'm going to Georgetown, you silly," answered Linda. "That's a big city. I'll probably not even see a mountain."

Everyone waved and smiled. Betsy tried her best to smile with her mouth closed, but it was pretty difficult. Dr. Madden had told Mom she must wait a bit before taking her to get braces, and now Betsy was more self-conscious than ever.

"I have a good idea," said Dorothy as they were driving home.

"Another play?" asked Julie.

"No. A newspaper. How would it be if we had a weekly newspaper to send to Linda?"

"That sounds like a lot of work," said Mona.

"You wouldn't have to do anything," replied Dorothy with irritation. She wanted everyone to be enthusiastic about her plan. "I'll be the chief reporter and the editor. You can all tell me the news, I'll write it up, and then we'll send it off. We could even send it to the aunts and uncles. They're always begging for news about the farm."

"Sounds fine to me," said Mom. "Then I wouldn't have to write all those letters."

During the next week they discussed the newspaper and what should be in the first issue.

"Will it have cartoons or comics?" asked Sara.

"If I can think of some," responded Dorothy. "But I'm not too good at drawing. We'd better save that for later."

"My favorite part of the paper is 'Dear Abby,'" said Carol. "I think you should have a column like hers."

"No," said Betsy. "'Dear Heloise.'" She tried reading "Dear Abby," but most of the time it was full of stupid things like boyfriends, and divorces and relatives who disagreed with each other. "Hints from Heloise" had much more practical information. After all, you never knew when you might have to keep bacon from sticking to the pan, or use cornstarch because you ran out of floor wax, or things like that.

"I'll combine them," decided Dorothy. "My column will be 'Dear Gladys,' and you can write for personal advice or to give household hints. I'll announce it in the first issue and then have the column starting with the second."

"Gladys! Why 'Dear Gladys?' We don't know anyone by that name," said Betsy.

"It just came into my head and I like it," retorted Dorothy. "But that's not enough to make a newspaper, even with headlines and feature articles. Mom, what do you always read in the paper, besides the front page?"

"The hospital report, the births, the weddings and the obituaries," answered Mom promptly.

"That's it!" cried Dorothy. "A column reporting all the animals that are born or take sick or die." Then she became silent a moment. Betsy felt sure Dorothy was thinking about their animal cemetery in the apple orchard. She hoped the newpaper wouldn't be too sad.

"What about us?" asked Julie. "I had a sliver in my finger today and Mom had to take it out. That's not going to the hospital, but it's something like it."

Dorothy swiftly wrote some notes. "Good point, Julie. We'll include things like that in the column. Linda will have to laugh when she reads it."

"And what if Sara and Teensie get into the dehorning paste again?" Betsy couldn't resist asking.

"They'd better not!" said Mom.

"I'd suggest a lost-and-found column," said Danny,

"but probably it would get kind of boring."

"Why?" asked Mom. "I think it's a good suggestion. I'm always losing things."

"That's what I meant," continued Danny. "Every week we'd have to report your glasses lost and found at least a dozen times."

Mom threw a potato peel at Danny, but he escaped out the front door.

When Dad came in that evening, Dorothy asked him, "What parts do you always read in the paper?"

"In winter I check the prices of pigs and steers, but pretty soon I'll have to start checking the price of hay if we don't get some hot weather. We're about to run out of bales, and none of the fields is quite ready to cut yet."

"Thanks, Dad! That's good for a short article." Again Dorothy wrote in her notebook. By the end of the week she had enough to cover two sheets. While she hand-lettered the columns on two stencils, she wouldn't let anyone watch her.

"What's it going to be called?" asked Betsy.

"That's part of the surprise," answered Dorothy.

Mom had the stencils run off in town, and then Dorothy distributed copies. Betsy's eyes swiftly took in the name at the top: *Willow Wind Warbler*.

"Dorothy is so clever," she thought. Their farm was called Willow Wind, and *Warbler* sounded pleasant and fitting as a name for their family newspaper. She could almost hear one of the birds in their willow trees, warbling the news to all who passed. It was fun to read about all the happenings on the farm, even though they weren't exactly new to her. On the second page she read the Hospital Report.

"I didn't know Helen's calf was sick," said Betsy.

"Well, now you do," replied Dorothy.

For the next three weeks Betsy helped collect stories, and once she submitted a letter to "Dear Gladys."

Each week the *Willow Wind Warbler* came out on Monday, and in every issue Betsy found at least one thing she hadn't known before.

"It really *is* a good newspaper," she complimented Dorothy.

In the third week in June she read some news on the front page of the *Warbler* that was truly riveting.

> Due to an excessively busy schedule, Mother Bork reports that she is considering asking for a delay in the late June and early July birthday celebrations.

"What do you mean, 'considering a delay?'" Betsy asked Mom. Her birthday was coming up soon, and she hadn't heard a thing about a delay in the celebration of it.

"I knew that would bring you running," said Mom. "That's why I asked Dorothy to put the notice in as a news item. I'm so tied up with the booth that I promised to manage for our church during Steamboat Days, I don't see how I can get around to all the birthday shopping as well. I was wondering if you wouldn't mind picking another day, later in July, to celebrate your birthday. Carol and Kristine and Sara said they didn't care. But if you insist on your real birthday, we'll manage somehow."

Betsy thought for a moment. Carol, Teensie and Sara had birthdays close to Christmas, and Mom had always let them choose a day in June or July to celebrate, if they wished, so that their birthday excitement wouldn't get lost in the hectic time of the holidays. But for her it was different. She had always celebrated her birthday on the right day. Yet she could see Mom was harassed, trying to get a hundred loaves of bread baked and frozen so they would be ready to be made into dozens of sandwiches for sale at the booth. And she was forever answering the telephone, assigning schedules to the various persons who called to volunteer.

"I'll pick a day in July, after Steamboat Days," Betsy finally said.

"That's my cooperative little girl!" Mom gave her a hug.

Betsy felt a bit ashamed, because while it was true she wanted to cooperate with Mom, the main reason she had decided to postpone her birthday was because of an idea that would benefit her more than Mom. She was going to ask for only one birthday present: braces for her teeth. She suspected that money was the real cause for the delay in getting them, and she felt it was more likely she could convince her parents she needed them if she made her appeal after Steamboat Days.

"I won't ask for another thing," Betsy promised herself. "And I'll help Mom as much as I can."

Beauty and the Beast

"I'm glad you named me Betsy, Mom."

"Well, I'm glad you're glad," said Mom as she steered the car carefully around the curves of the road. They were on their way to Winona, and while Mom shopped for food for the church booth, Betsy planned to go to the library and pick out books to read over the summer.

She had thought about her name because she intended to look for some more Betsy-Tacy books. After February, she had hoped to read them in order, but the titles she wanted had always been missing from the library shelves.

"Maybe in summer there won't be so many kids trying to read them," thought Betsy.

Mom pulled the car up to the side entrance of the library, and Betsy jumped out.

"'Bye. See you later." Betsy opened the library door, skipped down the three steps and walked straight to the "L" fiction looking for Lovelace. She couldn't believe her eyes. There was a whole shelf of Betsy-Tacy books!

"I'm going to take one of each and read them all, even the fat ones," she decided. Using the list printed inside one of the books, she lined up the titles and counted. There were ten in the series, just the number she was allowed to take out on her card. Then she paused.

"What if the librarian won't let me take so many Betsy-Tacy books?" Clutching the volumes in two stacks, Betsy walked to the charge-out desk. She watched anxiously as the woman pulled out the cards and stamped each book, but instead of saying anything, she merely gave Betsy a smile.

Betsy had more than an hour to wait before her mother would come to pick her up again, so she sat down at one of the tables near the door, opened the copy of *Betsy-Tacy*, and began to read.

She read intently for ten pages, forgetting she was in the library. When she came to page eleven, where the author described how the book Betsy looked, the real Betsy gave a squeal of surprise.

"I don't believe it!"

"Don't believe what?" asked the woman at the desk. Betsy looked up, blushed, and turned the other way, too embarrassed to reply. She reread the paragraph she had just finished. She *had* remembered that the book Betsy had light-brown hair, the same color as hers, but she *hadn't* remembered about the space between her two front teeth. Yet there it was, in black and white.

. . . her hair was good and curly when the rags were removed. It stood out in a soft brown fluff about her face, which was round with very red cheeks and a smile which showed teeth parted in the middle.

In the book, Betsy had so much fun with her friend Tacy that she didn't seem at all concerned about having a space between her two front teeth. Furthermore, nobody called her Bugs Bunny or said, "What's up, Doc?"

"People were probably nicer back in those olden times," thought Betsy, and she continued reading. She had finished more than half of *Betsy-Tacy* by the time Mom came to get her.

"Oh, good! You checked out more Betsy-Tacy books," said Mom.

"I got all ten of them," gloated Betsy, and then she gave a sigh of contentment. "Betsy is the best name, in books and for real." That reminded her, however, of the very real space between her teeth.

"Mom, how much will it cost to have the dentist move my teeth together again?" she asked.

"Goodness, what a change of subject. What made you think of that?"

Betsy didn't want to mention the paragraph she'd read in *Betsy-Tacy* because then Mom would probably say something like "There, you see! That Betsy has a smile which shows her teeth parted in the middle and she doesn't mind at all." So she mumbled something about "just wanting to know."

"It will cost a lot, I'm sure. But you heard Dr. Madden recommend we not do anything until you're a bit older."

"Sure, and by then my teeth will stick out a mile," lamented Betsy.

"Not more than a quarter of a mile, I think," said Mom, so seriously that Betsy had to laugh.

When they pulled up into the farmyard, Dorothy came running out of the house to help carry in the groceries.

"Mom, do you have a good recipe for papier-mâché?" she asked.

"A recipe? You don't need a recipe for papier-mâché," answered Mom. "Just put in flour and water and newspaper strips."

"I know, but how much water and flour?"

"Depends on what you're making. But don't sidetrack me now. Let's get these groceries in first."

They carried the grocery bags into the kitchen, and while Mom put the things away, Dorothy started in on her request again.

"How much will I need for a big head—bigger than a horse's? I've decided on my costume for the Steamboat Days Parade, and the head has to be made out of papier-mâché."

"What are you going to be, Dort?" asked Betsy excitedly.

"I'm not telling. I want it to be a surprise."

"Come on, tell me," pleaded Betsy. "I'll keep it a secret and I'll help you make it."

Dorothy quietly considered the offer for a few moments and then changed her mind about not telling.

"All right, you can help me, but don't tell the others. I'm going to be the Beast—you know, like in 'Beauty and the Beast.' And I've thought of the most *beastly* costume you can imagine."

Betsy gasped. Instantly, she pictured Dorothy behind a fierce-looking mask. "But who," she wondered, "will be Beauty?" And then the thought pierced her like a delicious tickle. "She's going to ask *me* to be Beauty! That's why she let me in on the surprise."

Betsy was already imagining herself walking beside Dorothy in the parade. Usually the contestants grinned broadly and waved to their friends and family lining the street.

"I'll smile with my mouth closed and look mysterious," planned Betsy. "After all, Beauty shouldn't have an open space between her front teeth."

Mom interrupted Betsy's thoughts with a question: "Who's going to be Beauty?"

Betsy beamed, forgetting to close her mouth. She looked up at Dorothy, waiting for confirmation.

"Julie is. We've worked it all out. She's going to wear that white ballet costume we found in the rummage sale."

Betsy burst into tears, and Mom and Dorothy looked at her, perplexed.

"What's the matter?"

"I know why you didn't choose me—it's my teeth. But I can smile with my mouth closed," said Betsy. "Please let me be Beauty, Dorothy."

"I can't," protested Dorothy. "I've already promised Julie. Besides, the costume fits her. That's why I picked her in the first place. It had nothing to do with your teeth."

Betsy turned away, trying to hide her tears, as she headed toward the stairs and her room.

"Wait a minute!" Mom grabbed her by the arm and pulled her to the telephone. "Betsy, I think maybe it is time after all to do something about your teeth. I'll call Dr. Madden right now and ask."

"You see! I told you it was my teeth," wailed Betsy.

With a sob she pulled away from Mom and ran upstairs. She didn't want to hear anything more about her teeth. She was never going to look in a mirror again, not ever, and she would always remember to smile with her mouth closed. No! Better yet, she would never smile again.

Yet at the end of the week, when Mom quietly told her they had an appointment with Dr. Shayner, the orthodontist, she went along without a murmur.

"Hmm!" said Dr. Shayner several times as he examined Betsy's teeth and then the X-ray pictures he had taken of them. "A simple case of diastema. I think a retainer will help quite a bit."

He brought out something that looked like a pink plastic turtle and showed it to Betsy and her mother.

"I'm going to make a cast of the upper part of your mouth, and then we'll make one of these for you. If you promise to wear it all day, every day, I think you'll be seeing that space narrow down to almost nothing in several months. And it should pull your teeth in a bit, too, so they'll line up nicely with the others."

The rubbery plastic felt funny when Dr. Shayner pressed it up against the roof of her mouth.

"Come back next week for a fitting," said Dr. Shayner. "We'll see if we can get it right the first time."

Betsy was so happy she almost tripped going down the stairs of the Choate Building. She was so content she forgot to pester Mom about clogs, even when they passed a window full of them on the ground floor of Choate's. In fact, she was so cheerful she forgot all about being mad at Dorothy and Julie.

"I'll help you," she offered that evening as Dorothy and Julie started for the summer kitchen.

"Good," Dorothy nodded. She brought out crepe paper that needed to be cut into short strips and then twisted and torn until it looked like the shaggy hair of a beast. As soon as Betsy and Julie had a pile of the strips ready, Dorothy pasted them onto the monstrous beast's head that she had constructed out of papier-mâché. It seemed to take hours to cover one small patch.

"Are you sure we'll get this done in time?", asked Julie skeptically.

"We still have about ten days," Dorothy reassured her.

The next week Betsy went to have her retainer fitted, and after filing it down a bit on one edge, Dr. Shayner pronounced it ready. He slipped it into place and gave her strict instructions on how to keep it—and her teeth —clean and free from sticky food. At first it felt tight in her mouth and she kept wanting to spit it out, but later she got used to it.

"No gum chewing!" ordered Dr. Shayner.

Betsy solemnly agreed. She would do everything just as Dr. Shayner suggested, and maybe by the time school came around again in two months, the space between her teeth would hardly be noticeable.

"Come on, we have to hurry," said Mom as they came out into the blinding sunshine of the street. "We're going to arrive later than the plane." They were going to the La Crosse airport to pick up Aunt Anne, who was spending several weeks of vacation at their house and at Grandma and Grandpa's.

They weren't late and neither was the plane. Within an hour they had dropped Aunt Anne at Grandma's house and then returned home to do chores. That evening, Betsy helped work on the Beast costume again.

They had completed the head and were now at work on a pair of Danny's old overalls, covering them with the same shaggy twists of crepe paper.

"I don't see how we'll ever get done in time," said Julie, shaking her head. "We only have three days left, besides today."

"It does go slow," agreed Dorothy with a sigh.

"Aunt Anne offered to help," said Betsy.

"You weren't supposed to tell her!"

"I know, but it sort of slipped out."

"Well, if she knows, then I guess she might as well help."

The next day, Aunt Anne was allowed to enter the summer kitchen.

"Oh!" she gasped when she saw the Beast's head sit-

ting on top of a barrel. Its large, staring eyes and fero-
cious-looking teeth gleamed white in the dusky light.
Then she saw the partly finished overalls, stuffed with
newspapers and propped up against an old chair like a
headless half-bear, half-man. "That is a truly bestial costume!" she exclaimed.

"It's not finished yet," explained Dorothy.

"I sort of like it the way it is," said Aunt Anne. "It's as
though the Prince were halfway out of his spell."

"A prince wouldn't be wearing overalls," said Dorothy, disgusted that Aunt Anne couldn't see something so
obvious. "No, he has to be completely covered with the
crepe-paper fur."

"All right, you're the boss," said Aunt Anne.

They worked feverishly that day and the next, stop-
ping only to eat and do their chores. At last the costume
was ready.

"It's done." Dorothy sighed with relief. "Now I have a
day to practice moving like a Beast."

"I think I'll wait to see the full effect in the parade,"
said Aunt Anne.

The morning of the parade dawned clear and cloud-
less. That was one of the many good things about Steamboat Days, Betsy decided. They were always held in
early July, when it hardly ever rained during the day.

Mom took Dorothy and Julie to town in the pickup,
with the costumes spread out carefully in the back, under an old sheet. The girls would get dressed in the
Farmer's Exchange, where Dad worked, and then walk
the block to the starting point of the parade.

"Is everybody ready?" called Kathy. She was driving
the rest of the family in the car.

After parking, they hurried to the spot on Main Street

where they had agreed to meet Grandma, Grandpa and Aunt Anne. Soon Mom came rushing up.

"It should start in a few minutes," she said. "Dorothy and Julie are about midway in the lineup."

The words were barely out of her mouth when they heard the sounds of a band. Around the starting corner came the St. Stan's marchers, trim and neat in their red-and-white uniforms. Following them was a parade of children of every age and description: riding bicycles trimmed with fluttering crepe paper; guiding prancing ponies and horses with saddles flaunting colorful pom-poms; pushing doll and baby carriages decked out with ribbon rosettes and garlands of flowers; pulling wagons decorated with slogans and drapery; walking in costumes that ranged from space suits to Superman.

As each one passed by, the crowd applauded, and sometimes the little children sitting in the carriages or wagons blew kisses back to the onlookers.

"Isn't she sweet!"

"What a darling!"

"How cute!"

Betsy listened to the comments of the parade viewers, and a nervous tightness spread through her chest, as though she were holding her breath, but she wasn't. She was wondering whether Dorothy and Julie would compare favorably with all this competition, but she did not allow the thought to develop further.

Far down the line, Betsy heard shrieks and squeals. Stepping off the curb for a moment, she peered down the street. A lumbering bearlike monster was moving toward a group of children in the crowd, thrusting out a fiendish snout and growling fiercely. The smaller children hid their faces against their parents, while the older ones danced up and down, shivering with excitement as they stepped out and poked fingers at the beast, ready to scamper back to the safety of the curb when it turned on them with a snarl.

"It's Dorothy!" yelled Betsy. It had taken her some moments to realize it; her sister looked and acted so strange in the costume.

The crowd laughed and applauded as Dorothy, the Beast, approached Julie, the Beauty. Julie quivered and quaked, then pretended to faint. At that, the Beast turned with a grunt and moved toward the curb where people were laughing the loudest. The bellows and roars that Dorothy let out echoed in the hollow head and sounded much more ferocious than any human voice. Betsy was sure that some of the children were convinced there really was a beast of some sort inside the monstrous costume.

When the parade was over, the family walked to the church booth where Mom had to check up on supplies of food and drink. They waited there, munching on sandwiches and sipping soft drinks. Dorothy and Julie were coming to meet them as soon as they had a chance to walk past the judging stand to see the names of the winners posted.

"You were sensational," said Aunt Anne to Dorothy the moment she appeared, carrying her Beast head under one arm.

"The judges didn't think so," said Dorothy. "They only gave us fourth prize."

"Fourth prize?" Aunt Anne was astonished. "I can't believe that. Yours was the most original costume in the entire parade."

"Well, it's true," said Julie. "We got fourth prize. But I

could care less. All I want is a tall, tall drink of something cool."

"Me, too," said Dorothy. She tried to appear as indifferent as Julie, but it was obvious she was crushed.

"This is what I hate about children's contests," Betsy heard Aunt Anne mutter to Grandma. Then she turned to speak to Dorothy. "Sometimes judges make mistakes because they can't see the whole picture," she explained. "They probably didn't even get a chance to see you in action with the crowd. But take my word for it—you were the best."

"If I were the best I would have had first prize," said Dorothy abruptly.

"I told you—judges can make mistakes," insisted Aunt Anne. "And it's not what the judges say that counts. It's what you feel and know to be the truth. You try to stand off and see yourself objectively, and sometimes you can say, 'I was the best.' It doesn't happen often. Most of the time, even when those who are judging say you were the best, you know inside yourself you could have done better. But once in a while, like today, you can honestly say 'I was the best' and it shouldn't matter what anyone else says or thinks."

"Well, if you ask me," said Betsy, "I think we had the most fun we ever had at one of these parades. Dorothy, did you see that little kid squeal when you brushed your arm against her face? And the one who put his finger in your mouth—I thought he'd wet his pants when you caught hold of it and sucked on it! And did you notice how some of them came to help Julie get up? You were really good, too, Julie—that looked just like fainting."

"Oh, Betsy, I love you," said Aunt Anne, giving her a hug. "You say it so much better than my preaching."

Birthday Bonfire

On the Monday after Steamboat Days were over, Betsy handed Mom her birthday wish list:

No. 1. A pair of clogs
No. 2–10. Surprises

She was supposed to put ten things on her list, but now that she had her retainer, the only thing she really wanted was a pair of clogs. It was not likely she would get them, she knew, yet it never hurt to keep asking.

"You still haven't told me what day you want us to celebrate," said Mom.

"I haven't decided yet," answered Betsy, "but I will—soon."

During the week the family worked hard clearing out the old brooder house. Dad was going to replace it with a new one, so they had to take out all the feeding trays and drinking cups that were still good. At first, Dad thought he could salvage some of the lumber, but when he tried to take it apart, it crumbled or cracked in every spot where a nail had been.

"It's totally rotted out. We'll do better to burn it down and start fresh," he said. He wanted to set it on fire that evening, but Dorothy prevailed upon him to wait.

"Let's have a big bonfire on Sunday night! A giant one. Inside the shed we'll put all the old things we want to burn, and then we'll dance around it." Dorothy had read about Midsummer celebrations, and even though Midsummer Eve had already passed, the bonfire seemed like a terrific idea. Betsy could hardly believe it when Dad agreed. As soon as he had, she ran to Mom.

"I want my birthday to be on Sunday."

"But we're having a family picnic then, at Perrot Park, don't you remember? Fran and Mickey are coming for the weekend."

"Can't it be my birthday, too? We could have the cake at the picnic. I'd like that," Betsy insisted.

"If that's the way you want it, we'll see what we can do," said Mom.

When Sunday arrived, everyone felt jolly and cooperative as they went to early Mass, hurried through the outside chores, prepared the picnic lunch and collected the bats, softball, volleyball, net and other paraphernalia that made a picnic so much fun.

"Hurry," Betsy urged everyone. "We want to get a table in a good spot."

"Don't worry," Carol assured her. "Uncle Robert and

Aunt Nettie are coming, too, and their kids will know enough to hold at least three tables for this big bunch."

"It's getting better and better," thought Betsy. "Now there are enough persons to make two good softball teams."

They started the game as soon as they arrived at the park. On each team were some older, bigger children and some smaller, younger ones. When Danny or Mona or one of the older children stepped up to bat, the out-fielders moved far back, but when Betsy or one of her younger sisters or cousins took a turn, everyone ran forward, closer to the infield.

"Once, just once, I'd like to send that ball flying past them," thought Betsy as she selected a bat and walked toward the plate. Maybe it was because she was celebrating her birthday and on your birthday you're supposed to get a wish fulfilled; or maybe it was the glorious weather that gave her an extra lift; or perhaps it was just plain luck—Betsy didn't know and she didn't stop to think about it. All she knew was that suddenly her bat connected with the ball in exactly the right way, and the ball flew. Around the bases she ran, hearing her team-mates yelling and prompting.

"Go for third, Betsy! Go for third!"

"No, go for home! Go for home!"

Her right foot touched the edge of third base, and without slowing down, she pivoted and headed in one smooth motion for the home plate. The pounding in her chest matched the rhythmic thuds of her feet.

"Faster, Betsy, faster!"

"You'll make it!" someone shrieked.

And she did. It was the first home run she ever had.

"Nothing can spoil my birthday now," she thought as

she flopped, deliriously happy, onto the grass next to her teammates.

The score kept going back and forth. First one team would be ahead and then the other. It was at a tie when Mom called from the tables.

"Come and eat."

Betsy realized she was famished, and immediately lost interest in the game. They could finish it later if they wanted to.

"Mom, where's your purse?" she asked as she came running up to one of the long tables. "I need a safe place to put my retainer while I eat."

"I didn't bring one," said Mom. "But I think Aunt Anne did. Put it in hers."

Betsy looked around for some waxed paper to wrap around her retainer, but couldn't see any. Then she spotted two bubble-gum wrappers that her cousins had left on a corner of the table.

"I'll use these. Afterward my retainer will taste like bubble gum," she thought.

Slipping the retainer out of her mouth, Betsy folded the two gum wrappers around it. She looked around for Aunt Anne but didn't see her. However, her purse was propped up on one of the benches, so Betsy tucked the wrapped retainer inside. Looking up, she saw Aunt Anne coming across the field from the direction of the water pump, carrying two pitchers.

"I put something in your purse," Betsy called out to her. "For safekeeping."

Then she took her place in line by the grill where Uncle Fran had cooked the hamburgers and bratwurst until they were just right: crisp and crunchy on the outside and tender on the inside. She filled her plate with potato salad, gelatine salad, baked beans, carrot sticks, olives and pickles and then munched and chewed in contentment, while all around her the rest of the family and relatives did likewise.

"Don't forget there's birthday cake," said Mom.

Everyone groaned, but no one left the tables, except Aunt Anne.

"I've got to walk off some of this food before I'll have room for cake," she said. "Besides, I need a wash. I'm full of pickle juice. Julie, tuck my purse under my arm, will you, so I won't get it sticky."

Betsy almost called out, "Watch out for my retainer!" But she was busy chewing on an olive, and before she had spit out the pit, Aunt Anne was gone.

At the far table, Mom took the birthday cake out of a box and Betsy pretended not to see as she arranged the candles on top. As soon as Aunt Anne returned, someone lighted the candles and everyone sang:

> Happy Birthday to you;
> Happy Birthday to you;
> Happy Birthday, dear Betsy;
> Happy Birthday to you!

Mom carried the cake to Betsy's table and set it down in front of her. It was covered with fudge frosting, and the candles were placed on it in the shape of a number nine. Silently she made her wish: "I want the space between my teeth to be gone before school starts." Then she blew the candles out on her first try. Kathy cut the cake, and in a few minutes Betsy's tongue wound around that dark, velvety goodness.

"Now for the presents," said Mom, putting a pile of wrapped packages in front of Betsy.

From Mom and Dad and her family, Betsy got useful things like new socks and underpants and fun things like a new jump rope, a painting set, a picture puzzle and green bath oil in a bottle shaped like a fish. Her grandparents gave her a skirt that Grandma had made, and from Aunt Anne she got books, as usual. Betsy was happy with all her presents, but secretly thought the best one was the home run, and she had given that to herself. But she politely said nothing.

"Who wants to go for a walk up Brady's Bluff?" asked Dorothy. It was a scary climb, because there were many rattlesnake nests in the rocks, or so people said. They had never actually met up with a rattlesnake, even though they climbed Brady's Bluff each time they came to Perrot Park for a picnic. From the top it was possible to see far up and down the Mississippi River.

"I'll go," said Betsy. "But first I have to put in my retainer." She went to rinse her mouth out with water as Dr. Shayner had taught her and then walked to Aunt Anne's side.

"I put my retainer in your purse and now I want it back."

"You did?" asked Aunt Anne.

"Yes. I put it right in here." Betsy zipped open the central part of the purse and peered in. She could see no sign of her retainer.

"Betsy, when did you put it there?" asked Aunt Anne.

With a sinking feeling, Betsy replied, "Just before I called out to you. Didn't you hear me?"

"No, I didn't hear what you said, exactly." Aunt Anne looked as though she had a headache or a pain. "What did it look like?"

"It's a pink plastic thing. I wrapped it in two bubble-gum wrappers," explained Betsy, really worried now. What could Aunt Anne have done with her retainer?

"Betsy, I have a dreadful confession to make. I threw away your retainer."

"You threw it away? Why did you do that?"

"I thought it was a wad of chewed bubble gum that someone had dropped into my purse to be funny, so I threw it away."

"Where?"

"In one of those big garbage cans, there, next to the building." Both Betsy and Aunt Anne swerved their eyes to the line of fat, tall metal barrels. There were at least ten of them.

"Could we look for it?" asked Betsy hopefully.

"Yes, I suppose we could." Aunt Anne got up from the bench.

"Hurry, Betsy, we're about to start off for Brady's Bluff," said Rob.

"Oh, no, you're not," said Aunt Anne. "You're about to go searching for a retainer in some garbage. I hereby deputize you all as Search Assistants, First Class."

There were groans and protests, but once Aunt Anne explained, they agreed to try.

"Which one did you throw it in?" asked Betsy as they came near the garbage barrels.

"That's the trouble. I remember throwing it in this direction but I haven't the faintest notion where it landed."

First they looked all around the barrels, but there was no sign of the retainer. There was nothing left to do but start digging through the garbage.

"I'm almost sure I threw it toward the first three," said Aunt Anne. "We'll transfer the garbage from these into the empty one at the end."

Piece by piece they picked over the contents of the three cans: paper plates, bottles, cans, coffee grounds, apple cores, cake crumbs, half-eaten hot-dog buns, half-melted gelatine, olive pots, globs of ketchup, watermelon rinds, chicken bones, paper napkins—everything had to be stirred or squeezed or twisted to make sure the retainer was not stuck to it.

Now that she saw what her retainer had been thrown

among, Betsy wasn't so sure she wanted it back. "It will be covered with germs," she thought. "How will I ever get it washed clean?" But then she remembered how expensive it had been, and she knew Mom wouldn't buy her another one so soon.

"We've just got to find it," she said.

The searchers were coming close to the bottom of the three barrels.

"Yuck!" cried Rob. "I'm not digging any further."

Aunt Anne looked inside the barrel.

"Yuck is right. Let's stop. It's not worth it."

"Yes it is!" cried Betsy. "It cost a lot of money."

"I didn't mean it that way," said Aunt Anne. "It's just that I don't think you'd want to wear it after it had been in that."

Betsy took one swift look inside the barrel. The bottom layer of garbage was covered with squirming white maggots and slugs crawling over everything.

"I will never, ever wear my retainer again, if it got thrown in there," vowed Betsy. It was all she could do not to give up in despair. She had barely started getting her teeth to move together, and now they would probably spring back again.

"Don't worry, Betsy," said Aunt Anne. "I'll pay for a new retainer. I'll even call Dr. Shayner first thing tomorrow, to tell him it was my fault."

Betsy swallowed with relief. Yet, as she tramped along the path up to Brady's Bluff, she worried about the week's delay before she could get a new one. And it was still on her mind that evening as they prepared for the bonfire.

"Stand back, everyone," cried Dad as he threw a flaming piece of kindling into the center of the old brooder house. With a whoosh fire spread over the gasoline he had sprinkled there, burst into gigantic flames that leaped through a hole in the roof, and spurted upward, like the Old Faithful geyser Betsy had seen once on television.

Grasping hands, they formed a circle. Even the grown-ups joined in, all except Dad, who stayed by the hose, ready to turn it on in case cinders or chips flew too far away from the fire. First the circle moved right, and then left. Faster and faster they whirled, laughing and shrieking. Then, as if at some secret signal, they dropped each other's hands and continued dancing, but each in his or her own way.

Betsy felt as if the flaming tongues and sparks were sending shocks of electricity right through her, forcing her to twist and turn and leap until every muscle and bone in her body was twanging like a guitar string. She forgot about everything except the mad, wild dancing.

Suddenly, with a heavy sighing sound, the roof and walls of the brooder house caved in. For a while, the flames blazed higher than ever, and then slowly but surely they got lower and lower until finally the bonfire was only a few feet off the ground. The dancers came to the same slow stop, dropping one by one to sit at the edge and stare, hypnotized, into the glowing embers.

"Here are the marshmallows," called Mom softly, not wanting to break the spell.

They sat around for another hour, quietly toasting and eating marshmallows and watching the fire diminish to a heap of smoldering coals and ashes. Ever after, whenever she thought of her ninth birthday, Betsy remembered her lost retainer and her first home run, but mostly she recalled the glory of her birthday bonfire.

Taffy Pull

For a month, Betsy wore her new retainer every day, and every morning she looked hopefully at her teeth, searching for signs that they were growing closer together. She didn't see much difference in them, but six weeks later, when she had to visit Dr. Shayner again, he assured her the teeth had moved about a tenth of a centimeter closer. When Betsy looked that up on Kathy's special ruler, she could hardly see the space, it was so tiny.

"No wonder I can't notice it," she thought. Still, she was relieved to hear there was some progress.

She had finished reading the first four Betsy-Tacy books and had even read parts of them aloud to Sara and Kristine. Now Dorothy was continuing the stories by reading aloud to them every evening. They were in the middle of *Heaven to Betsy*.

"I suspected Betsy Ray was probably upset about the space between her teeth!" said Betsy after Dorothy read a chapter in which the book Betsy expressed dissatisfaction with her looks, especially her teeth "with the part in the middle." She wished she could reach across the years and hand Betsy Ray a retainer.

"I'm glad I live now," thought Betsy. "Olden days are fun to read about, but modern times are better to live in."

In the middle of August, Mike came to spend a week at the farm. He helped with the haying and combining, but there was also time for games every evening. Sometimes they played Flashlight Tag, and other times they played another kind of Tag called Ditch. Or, if they finished supper early and it wasn't too dark, they had softball games and all the neighbors' children joined in.

One evening it grew dark by seven and looked as though it might storm, so they stayed inside.

"I feel in the mood to make some candy," said Kathy.

"Fudge. Make fudge," suggested Betsy.

"No, I think I'll try my hand at some taffy. I've always wondered what it was like to pull taffy, and this seems like a good time to find out." Kathy was already removing some of the cookbooks from the shelf. "There are at least two recipes I'd like to try," she said after she had read through more than a dozen of them. "I'll make each in a different flavor: one mint and one vanilla." She gathered the ingredients on the table and set the children to measuring sugar, water and butter.

"Butter these all over, really well," said Kathy, placing two large platters on the table. While the sugar-and-water mixture heated up, Betsy slathered butter over the entire surface of one platter and Julie did the same with the other. It seemed quite a long time before the candy thermometer reached the temperature Kathy wanted.

"Everybody stand back. The book says you have to be careful not to splash, and I'm not going to pour this out unless you're all six feet away from the table."

It was hard to stand so far away when they wanted to be involved in every step of the candy-making process. They could barely see the syrupy liquid as Kathy poured it slowly over one of the platters, but they could smell the vanilla that she sprinkled over it.

"Okay, now you can come and look, but don't touch," said Kathy. "Let it cool while I put on the second batch."

They gathered around the table again. The taffy was spread out over the platter in a thick layer of golden smoothness. On one end it had dripped over the edge and six golden globules flattened out on the table, look-ing like the shiny polished stones Uncle Fran sometimes gave them. Betsy reached out to touch one, but Kathy's warning voice stopped her.

"I said don't touch! You could get a severe burn. Wait until I give the signal."

With a buttered scraper she began to work the taffy toward the center of the platter, twisting and turning it so that it would cool on all sides. Betsy watched her for a while, but her eyes kept straying to the drops of taffy on the table. Surely those were cool enough to pick up and eat. Mike must have had the same idea because he touched one of them lightly with his forefinger.

"It's cool," he said.

"All right," said Kathy with a laugh. "You can each have one of the pieces that dripped over the side."

Betsy scraped up one of the circles of taffy and was

about to pop it into her mouth when she remembered her retainer and slipped it out. She set it on the table next to the empty platter and then put the taffy ball into her mouth. It was still quite warm, but luckily not so hot it burned. With her tongue, Betsy worked the chewy, sticky mass around behind her teeth. It was delicious, even though it was difficult to manage.

"I think this is ready to pull," said Kathy to Mike. "Do you want to try it?" Nobody minded that he got to be first because he was company.

"Butter your hands and then pick it up and start stretching it," Kathy instructed.

Mike did as he was told and then suddenly gave a howl.

"Ow! This is still hot!" He flung the taffy toward the platters, but it missed, landing half on a platter and half on the table.

"I'm sorry, Mike," said Kathy. "It felt cool enough to me. But now you see what I mean." She buttered her own hands and began scraping the taffy into a ball again.

"Good heavens, what's this?" she exclaimed as a big lump showed up in the taffy.

Betsy took one look and knew immediately it was her retainer.

"I don't believe it!" she cried. "Why do these things always keep happening to me?"

"If you'd put it in a safe place, nothing would go wrong," said Kathy as she separated out the glob of taffy containing the retainer. "Here, take it and wash it under warm water, almost hot. And, Mike, you start pulling now because it's time for me to pour the second batch."

Betsy took the lump of taffy into the bathroom. She felt she'd rather clean up the retainer there, so the others wouldn't be watching her.

"Well, at least it's not garbage, but good-tasting candy," she thought. She almost changed her mind and licked away the taffy but decided that wasn't such a good idea. Then a dreadful suspicion began to seep into her. What if the taffy had been so hot it had melted the retainer out of shape?

In an agony of suspense, Betsy held it under a stream of warm water, rubbing gently so as to melt away the hardening taffy. When the retainer was at last completely free of candy, Betsy slid it into place in her mouth.

"Does it feel extra tight or is that my imagination?" she wondered, moving her tongue experimentally over the retainer's surface.

"I just can't go back to Dr. Shayner again so soon," she thought. Even though Aunt Anne had telephoned him when the first retainer was lost, he had wanted to hear the full story from Betsy and it had been truly embarrassing to explain in detail how her retainer had been thrown away in the garbage. Now she would have to tell a ridiculous tale about pulling taffy. No, it was really too much to bear!

All the while the children took turns pulling taffy, Betsy couldn't enjoy herself. She kept testing with her tongue to make sure her retainer felt all right. She didn't try any more taffy for fear it would stick to her teeth and stay hidden in the cracks and crevices even after she brushed them. That would surely make her retainer feel wrong. She went to bed still undecided as to whether or not the retainer had been bent out of shape.

In the morning it felt the same as it always had.

"At least, I think it does," Betsy reassured herself. Anyway, she was not going to call Dr. Shayner for a special visit. She would wait and see what he said the next time she was scheduled for a checkup.

The next week, in the excitement of Linda's return, she almost forgot about the retainer problem. Hearing Linda describe all the strange new things she had seen gave Betsy a thrill, but she was glad Linda was back home, safe and sound. Linda didn't stay long, though, because her college classes started before Labor Day, and in a flurry of unpacking, washing clothes and repacking, she was off before Betsy got to ask all the questions she had.

The other children were busy, too, getting their clothes and books and pencil cases ready for school. Mom bought them each a new pair of shoes, but no clogs.

"I didn't think she would change her mind," sighed Betsy.

Halloween Hobos

Before she had to see Dr. Shayner again, Betsy had a much more difficult encounter to live through. She feared it would be awkward to face her fourth-grade classmates, especially Jimmy, and have them see her take her retainer out to eat lunch at school. But it didn't turn out that way at all.

Jimmy did say something mean and teasing the first time he observed her remove the retainer.

"A turtle! Look at the turtle Betsy keeps in her mouth," he squealed.

"It's not a turtle, it's a retainer, and at least it keeps my tongue from always tattling the way yours does," Betsy snapped at him. She didn't know where that retort came from, and she didn't dream it would have the result it did: Jimmy looked at her in surprise and moved off to another group of classmates.

"Betsy has the neatest thing. It's a retainer and it stays in her mouth without glue or anything." He began seriously explaining to them about what he had just seen and his voice didn't sound one bit teasing.

"Let me see, Betsy."

"Show us how it works."

"Does it hurt?"

"How long do you have to wear it?"

Her classmates peppered her with questions and Betsy answered them all. She was a little embarrassed at being the center of so much attention, but they really seemed to want to know all about her retainer.

"I wish I could have a retainer," said one of the girls. "You're probably going to end up with beautiful teeth. You could even be a model, maybe."

Betsy wasn't sure her teeth would be as beautiful as all that, but it was nice to know at least one classmate thought so. And she was tremendously relieved to find out she could openly take her retainer out and put it back in again without having to be secretive for fear of being made fun of.

At the next session with Dr. Shayner, before she could mention the taffy accident and ask whether the retainer was out of shape, he told her it was time to get a new one because her teeth were moving together so rapidly they had given her mouth a different shape.

"All that worry for nothing!" thought Betsy.

Still, she was concerned about her new retainer because of what she had heard about disasters coming in sets of threes. She had endured two of them and wondered when the third one was likely to befall her.

"Mom, is it true about bad things always coming in threes?"

"What do you mean?"

"You know. When there's a plane accident, and then another, everybody waits and says there'll be a third one for sure."

"That's just superstition," Mom reassured her.

"Well, why do accidents seem to happen so often in threes, then?"

"I'm sure some are caused by people thinking so much about another accident they get nervous or careless and so it really happens. If they would calm down a bit and think straight, they wouldn't be so influenced by the power of suggestion."

After that, Betsy tried hard not to think about any more awful things that could happen to her retainer. Instead, she was extra careful about putting it in a safe place whenever it was out of her mouth.

October came and she began to worry more about something else, and that was Halloween. Mom didn't let the children go out on Halloween unless they went with a friend from town, in a familiar neighborhood. Betsy had never gone trick-or-treating, and she was hoping that one of her classmates would invite her. Dorothy was going with a friend and would wear her Beast costume again. Julie had been asked by a classmate to spend the night. But so far no one in her class had asked Betsy what she was doing on Halloween, which was on a Friday this year.

"Don't they realize it's impossible to go trick-or-treating when you're on a farm?" she commented peevishly to her mother one day.

"Why not ask Christie outright if you can go along with her?" suggested Mom.

Betsy didn't want to do that. She wanted to be invited without having to beg. But as Halloween drew near, and she still had no invitation, she asked Christie one day, "What are you doing for Halloween?"

"I'm invited to my cousin's place in Goodview," Christie answered. "It's really great out there. They load you down with candy in almost every house."

Betsy sighed. She could hardly expect Christie to invite her to her cousin's house. Now she was sure that another Halloween would pass and she still wouldn't know what it was like to trick-or-treat.

It was Grandma, not one of her classmates, who finally came up with an invitation when she called on the telephone one day.

"Betsy, would you like to stay over on Friday night and go trick-or-treating with Robert? He's coming to spend the weekend and I don't think he should go out by himself."

"Yes, Grandma! Yes! Yes! Yes!" shouted Betsy.

"What am I going to wear?" she yelped as soon as she hung up. It had not seemed necessary to plan for a costume until she was sure she would need it.

"I think Aunt Mickey said Rob was bringing a hobo outfit of some sort. You could be a pair of hobos," suggested Mom.

The more Betsy thought about it, the better she liked the idea. It was not babyish and it would be easy to make. And when Dad brought out one of his big red flowered handkerchiefs and showed her how to tie it at the end of a pole, making a container suitable for the treats they would collect, Betsy was convinced they would have the best costumes of anyone in the fourth grade. There would be no need for a plastic jack-o'-lantern such as the ones she had seen the first-graders carrying around.

"Take my flashlight if you want to," Dad offered. "Only be sure to bring it back."

When getting dressed at Grandma's on Halloween, Betsy slung the strap of the flashlight over her head and one shoulder. Then she put on the tattered coat Mom had helped her find in the attic. If she put her hand into the right pocket and reached through the hole in it, she could snap on the flashlight and direct its beam either to her own face or on someone standing in front of her.

Betsy and Rob set out, walking in the direction of the big houses on Broadway. On the corners the street lamps

shone brightly, but in the middle of each block was a dark area that caused a shivery feeling to run down her back whenever they stopped to ring a doorbell or open a gate. The huge tree trunks and the almost-bare branches took on queer shapes, as though they could only be seen for what they were under cover of darkness.

"It's like being on the edge of something scary, and yet knowing you're safe," Betsy decided, for in the moments when the ghostly shadows seemed about to become most alarming, invariably a door would open and the front steps of a house would be lit up, and instead of dreadful creatures they saw only the most ordinary mothers or fathers, generously passing out candy or coins.

"Halloween is fun, but it's not spooky enough," complained Rob. "I went to a House of Horrors once, but even that wasn't very scary. It's too fake. I'd like to go to a really spooky place, where it wasn't made up by somebody. You know, like a house where nobody ever went, because they believed it was haunted. Or a deep, dark cave full of bones, or something like that."

"We have caves near our farm," said Betsy. "I don't know if they're full of bones, but I think they're deep and dark."

"You mean you never went inside them?"

"No, but the older kids did." Betsy didn't want to explain that she had been invited to go with them but had been too frightened.

"Why didn't they ever tell me about them?" asked Rob. "Come on, let's go home and tell ghost stories to each other, about all the people whose bones are in the caves."

"I told you, I don't know if there are any bones," said

Betsy, but she agreed to go back to Grandma's house. They were due back soon, anyway.

Upstairs in the dark, Rob lay in his sleeping bag on the floor and made up stories about outlaws and bank robbers who might have hidden out in the caves. Betsy lay in the bed and pulled the blankets over herself tightly.

"Let's go inside one of the caves tomorrow," whispered Rob.

"Okay," Betsy answered, but secretly she hoped he would forget about them. However, the next day he brought up the subject again as soon as he and Betsy arrived at the farm.

"You may *not* go to those caves alone," ordered Mom after she had seen Rob and Betsy put some of their Halloween candy into a sack, set off by themselves, and then asked them where they were going. They went in search of Dorothy and talked her into going along.

"Have you got the flashlight?" she asked as they were already on the way.

"Do we need it?" asked Betsy.

"Yes," insisted Dorothy. "I wouldn't go near those caves without a flashlight."

Betsy ran to get one while Dorothy and Rob waited. After this slight delay it didn't take long to arrive at the bluff where the caves were located. The mouths of the caves were low and narrow.

"Those two are nothing much," said Dorothy as Rob poked his head into the first two holes and then backed out again. "That one over there is the big one."

They crouched on hands and knees, wiggling past the weeds that covered the cave's mouth. Inside, there was only the faintest of light, but it was strong enough to show that the cave was quite large—as big as a room.

Dorothy reached to pull forward the flashlight strapped on her back but Rob stopped her.

"Let's sit and eat candy while you tell us a ghost story." Without waiting for an answer, he pulled a candy bar out of the bag and began munching. The odor of chocolate overwhelmed the damp, earthy smell of the cave.

Betsy was about to do likewise when she remembered her retainer. It was in her fingers, ready to come out, when she was reminded of something else.

"The third disaster!" she thought. "This could be it." She popped the retainer back into place.

"I'm not hungry now," she said, refusing the sack of candy bars Rob was holding out to her. She was not going to risk losing her retainer in the dark dust of the cave. No way!

Dorothy began a story about stolen gold and other treasures hidden away in the cave by robbers. She related how one by one they had been killed off, but their ghosts stayed in the cave, protecting it against others who might come to steal the treasure. As she stopped for a moment at a particularly spooky part, the silence in the cave was broken by a soft slithering sound.

"What's that?"

"Sssh!"

They listened again, not moving a muscle. The sound was repeated, like a rake scratching in the soil.

"It's probably a rat or a mouse," whispered Dorothy, as she carefully and quietly pulled the flashlight to the front of her chest.

"A rat or a mouse?" squeaked Betsy. She was used to seeing such animals in the barns or open fields, but having one in a cave with you was another matter.

But it was something much more dangerous than a rat or a mouse. As Dorothy shone the beam of the flashlight into the corner from which the noise had come, a soft rattle whirred and they saw a head stick up, and a forked tongue dart in and out.

"A rattlesnake!" breathed Dorothy.

Rob and Betsy were much too frightened to speak.

"I think the beam from the flashlight will hold him in place," whispered Dorothy shakily. "Ease over to the hole very slowly."

Inch by inch they crept toward the dim outline of the cave's mouth. Dorothy moved the slowest, trying not to let the flashlight waver and keeping the rattlesnake's head right in the center of the beam.

Betsy came out first, then Rob, and at last Dorothy. For a moment they stood there, trembling, and then they ran toward home as fast as they could go, heaving and gasping all the way. At the house they dropped to the steps, looking at each other in amazement.

"When I think of the number of times we crawled in there during the summer . . ." Dorothy shuddered at the memory.

"Don't snakes hibernate in winter?" asked Rob. "It probably went into the cave recently."

"I think we should put a warning by that cave so no one else goes in," said Dorothy.

Betsy agreed, but she didn't exactly look forward to a return to the caves. She didn't want to go anywhere near them for a long time.

"We'll be careful," said Dorothy.

"I'm willing," said Rob, and once he showed his bravery, Betsy decided she had to go along.

They took a small brush and a can of red paint. While Dorothy painted a sign on a rock, Betsy and Rob, armed with long sticks, kept on the lookout.

"Death to all who enter here!" stated the sign. Above the words Dorothy sketched the outline of a snake and below them a skull and crossbones.

"That should keep people out," she said, pushing the stone close to the mouth of the cave, and then running away.

"Am I ever glad Mom told me about being careful so as to avoid the third accident," reflected Betsy. The very thought of her retainer lying on the ground in the cave with the rattlesnake gave her the shivers.

Heart Attack

The close call in the cave worked like a charm on Betsy.

"After all," she thought, "if there is anything to that superstition about threes, I can say I've passed my three."

She stopped fretting about her retainer and took it so much for granted that on her November visit, when Dr. Shayner pointed out she was more than halfway there in her effort to close the space between her teeth, Betsy could only look in the mirror in wonder.

"Why didn't I notice it?" she cried. The space had narrowed down to a fairly thin line.

Life in the fourth grade began to be full and exciting. Her classmates were all friendly and cooperative, and her teacher, Miss Lanzoni, was always coming up with unusual ideas for social studies. Right now the class was making maps. Betsy was trying to draw their farm on a big sheet of white paper, showing all the roads, paths and fields, with symbols for each of the different buildings and crops.

"This ruler keeps sliding around so much I can't get the lines straight. Why don't they make a ruler that stays where you put it?" Betsy complained mildly, but she really meant it to be funny. She was in a merry mood and wanted to share it with the other members of her family.

"Why don't you invent one? It might make you a millionaire," commented Danny.

Ordinarily, Betsy would have taken such a response in the wrong way, thinking Danny was needling her, but tonight she only smiled at him and continued working on her map.

"My word! Did you read this in the paper about the giant pumpkin grown on a farm near Arcadia? They're going to make pies out of it and hope to make over a hundred!" Mom read the short article aloud.

"Heavens to me!" cried Betsy.

"What did you say?" asked Mom.

"Ever since we read that one Betsy-Tacy book you're always exclaiming 'Heavens to Betsy!' I can't very well say that, since I am Betsy, so I say 'Heavens to me!'"

Mom chuckled and Danny groaned, but Carol laughed out loud.

"That's funny, Betsy. Why don't you use it as your personal expression?"

"I think I will," she announced, and turned back to

her mapmaking. For a few minutes, all was silence as each family member read or wrote or studied quietly.

"Ouch!" Betsy accidentally jabbed her arm with the sharp point of the pencil. "Oh, Heavens to me!" she said dramatically. "I poked a pencil into my skin. Do you suppose I'll get lead poisoning?"

"I know the symptoms," said Carol. "You'll start getting drowsy and weak. Then your stomach will be upset and you'll start vomiting and finally you'll have convulsions and go into a coma."

"I don't think I've got lead poisoning," said Betsy hastily.

Her ruler fell to the floor, and she twisted down and around in her chair, reaching to pick it up. But she lost her balance, and instead of the ruler, her hand grasped a chair spoke while her foot swung around and smacked against one of the table legs. A pain shot through her ankle, causing her to double up.

"Did you hurt yourself?" asked Mom.

"No," said Betsy when she had caught her breath, "but I hit my crazy bone in the ankle."

"What?" laughed Mom. "I never heard of such a thing."

"I never did, either," said Betsy, rubbing her ankle, "but it felt exactly the way it feels when you hit the crazy bone in your elbow, so I must have one in my ankle, too."

"You are something else," snorted Danny, shaking his head.

Betsy put away her map and began to read her social-studies book. She hadn't read more than five minutes when a broad grin broke out on her face.

"Did you know that pop is made from coal?" she

asked of no one in particular.

"Now what nonsense are you concocting?" asked Mom.

"It says right here that coke is made from coal," replied Betsy sweetly.

"Betsy, you're a regular little comedian tonight, aren't you?" laughed Mom. "Are you trying to give Uncle Ed a run for his money?"

Before Betsy could respond, the telephone rang. She raced to answer it but Carol got there first. With a stricken look, Carol handed the phone to Mom.

"It's Grandma," she whispered. "Grandpa has had a heart attack."

Mom didn't talk long and as soon as she was finished she put on her coat.

"I'm going to the hospital," she said. "Grandpa is in intensive care. I'll call you if anything happens."

The children continued sitting in the dining room, reading or doing their homework, but hardly saying a word.

"Here I was, laughing and joking while Grandpa was having a heart attack," Betsy thought, feeling a little strange.

"Come on, Betsy, Sara, Kristine," said Kathy. "Bedtime."

"I don't want to go to bed," said Betsy. "I couldn't sleep if . . ." She was afraid to finish the sentence. She didn't want to be sleeping if Grandpa died; she wanted to be awake and thinking about him.

"We'll wake you if we hear any news," promised Kathy.

Betsy stayed kneeling and praying longer than usual, and she continued her prayers after she had climbed into bed. She was sure she would not be able to sleep, and yet, before she knew it, it wasn't night anymore, but morning, and Mom was calling them to get up.

"Did you see Grandpa?" Betsy asked.

"Yes, I stayed until after midnight. It was a severe attack, but the doctors think he'll pull through," said Mom, wiping away a few tears of relief.

When Kathy left for school that morning in her own car, she carried a suitcase as well as her books.

"Where are you going?" asked Betsy in alarm.

"Mom thinks Grandma should have someone staying with her all the time, so I'm moving in with her."

"For good?" asked Betsy.

"For awhile, anyway."

"Does it have to be you?" Betsy got along best with Kathy, and it was discomforting to think she would no longer be there to smooth out the everyday squabbles the younger children were always having.

"I'm the only one available," said Kathy. "Linda is away at school, Danny can't do it with the schedule he has at Winona Tech, Carol has to drive you back and forth every day, and Mona's still too young to have a license. Grandma needs someone to drive her around. I'm glad I can help her out," she added. "In fact, it will be a lot better for me to live in town because I can get to the chemistry lab whenever I want."

After a week in the hospital, Grandpa came home, looking tired and gray. When the children visited or stayed overnight, he no longer teased them by trying to kiss them with a face full of shaving cream. Most of the time he sat in his chair or took short walks around the block.

Betsy tried to cheer him up whenever it was her turn to spend an afterschool period or an evening keeping him company while Grandma went shopping or to her church circle.

"Let's play checkers or cards, Grandpa," she would suggest.

"I'm not feeling too chipper today. Another day, perhaps," was his usual reply. It was sad and troubling.

Christmas was more cheerful, because Aunt Millie came home, bringing unusual gifts from Guyana.

"What is this?" asked Betsy as she opened a small box to find a lump of rough metal attached to a pin.

110

"It's raw gold," answered Aunt Millie. "It comes from those wild mountains Linda told me you were afraid of."

Betsy wasn't sure she'd ever wear the pin, but it certainly was a unique present and it would be fun to show her classmates. Luckily, Aunt Millie gave them each a ring as well, and Betsy's was of alexandrite. When she took it out of its tiny case it shone green against the white silk lining.

"Come here a minute," said Aunt Millie, taking Betsy into Grandma's bedroom where it was dark. She turned on a lamp and held Betsy's ring finger under it.

"Heavens to me!" exclaimed Betsy. "It's red now."

In the box she found a folded slip of paper that told all about alexandrite and explained why it changed color under artificial light.

"Listen, Grandpa," cried Betsy. "Wearing alexandrite is supposed to bring you health. And it's named after you: Alexander—alexandrite." She slipped her ring on Grandpa's little finger. It would be a pity to have to give up such a beautiful present, but if it really worked, maybe she should offer it to Grandpa.

"I have one of my own," said Grandpa, showing her a gold tie clasp Aunt Millie had given him, set with a stone of the same polished green.

Betsy smiled with relief, consoled by the thought that if there was some special power in alexandrite, it would be working on Grandpa, too.

"Wear it every day, Grandpa," she counseled him. "We want you to get well again."

Friday the Thirteenth

Grandpa did get better, but Betsy was sure it had nothing to do with the alexandrite, since he wore his tie clasp only on Sundays.

"Those things are just superstitions anyway," she reasoned, even though she liked the feeling she got when wearing her ring. And she had not had one runny nose or sore throat all January, when she usually suffered at least one bout with a cold.

"I didn't catch any because I'm happy, I guess," theorized Betsy. Grandma was always saying, "Happy people are healthy people," and Betsy tended to agree with her.

February was as cold and snowy as January, and still

Betsy stayed healthy and contented with life. Toward the end of the second week, Dad came in one evening and announced, "Full moon tomorrow. It will be clear and cold, so dress warmly."

"Full moon!" cried Carol. "And it's Friday the thirteenth, too."

"I wish you hadn't said that," said Dorothy. "We've got tests tomorrow and I'm sure to get flustered."

"Nothing can happen if you don't let it get to you," insisted Betsy. "Just pretend it's like any other day." She intended to sail through it, taking her usual precautions with her retainer, but without any special worry.

In the morning Danny came in late for breakfast, fussing and fuming. "Mom, call the milk hauler to come and empty the tank today instead of tomorrow. There's something wrong with the bulk tank again and I can't tinker with it until it's empty."

"Friday the thirteenth!" intoned Dorothy dramatically.

"Oh, pooh! Danny has been complaining about that tank for weeks now," said Betsy. "It just happened to break down today."

Sara came to the breakfast table and reached for the giant box of cereal at the exact moment Dad turned around with two pieces of toast from the toaster. Toast and Cheerios went flying in all directions.

"Friday the thirteenth!" squealed Kristine, but Dad did not think it was funny.

"Can't you be more careful?" he scolded Sara. Betsy thought this was not exactly fair because he had not looked, either, when he swung around.

They finished breakfast without further mishap, but on the way to the car Kristine refused to let anyone help her carry the large, three-dimensional cardboard collage she had painstakingly constructed over the past weeks, and it dropped to the snow as she tried to maneuver it and her armload of books.

"Yeah! Yeah! Friday the thirteenth to you, too!" taunted Sara, still angry with Kristine because she had refused to help pick up the scattered Cheerios.

"It's okay, Teensie, most of the stuff stayed on." Betsy tried to reassure her littlest sister because she knew how hard Kristine had worked at assembling the patches of cloth, pieces of bark, beans, tiny bolts, bits of foil and other oddments that made up her "texture sculpture," as she called it.

They brushed the snow away, and after Kristine got into the car, Betsy handed the collage to her.

"All in?" called Carol and she started up the car. They had made the turn onto the county road when there was a loud pop and the car swerved to the side of the road.

"If anyone mentions Friday the thirteenth, I'll scream," said Carol, clenching her teeth. She didn't have to get out of the car to confirm they had a flat tire, because the wobbly movement was familiar to all of them.

"Do you want me to run back and get Dad?" asked Julie.

"He left for work ahead of us this morning. You'll have to ask Mom to come on the tractor. I'm not even sure there's a jack in this car."

"Did you walk around and look at all the tires, the way you're supposed to before you get in?" asked Betsy.

Carol only gave her a disgruntled look.

"Cheer up," said Mom after she had brought the tools on the tractor and helped them change the tire. "That should be enough bad luck for any day."

And indeed, when they got home from school, the

only one to report any further misfortune was Dorothy.

"We were only allowed one pencil while we took all those tests and mine kept breaking," she groaned in recollection. "I'm sure Sister Helen thought I had a secret paper stashed in the sharpener and was trying to cheat."

"Never mind," laughed Mom. "I said before it was enough bad luck for the day, so let's stop thinking about it. Now help me get the house in order, because Linda's bringing her roommate, Janet, home for the weekend, remember? Betsy, you straighten up her room and vacuum it. Dorothy, you get out the good dishes and set the table. They'll be here in time for supper and I want it to look nice."

At six o'clock a car pulled into the yard and there was a boisterous welcome for Linda and Janet from the dogs, the children, and Mom and Dad.

"Mom, I hope you don't mind, but I brought *two* friends," said Linda, introducing another girl who had just stepped out from the back seat. "This is Suzanne."

"Hello, Suzanne. The more the merrier," said Mom with a smile. "Come in. We're almost ready to eat."

"Set another place at the table, Betsy," whispered Mom after they were all in the house again.

The family had gathered and sat down at the table, ready to say the prayer before meals, when Dorothy leaped up and began picking up her plate, cup and utensils.

"What's gotten into you?" asked Mom.

"You all may want to have thirteen sitting at the table on Friday the thirteenth, but I'm moving to the kitchen."

"Oh, stop that nonsense," laughed Mom. "We want you to sit here with the rest of us."

"Don't forget the full moon," said Dad with a wink.

"I just know something dreadful is going to happen," muttered Dorothy.

"Yes, it will if you keep thinking about it," said Mom, arranging a hot pad on the table. She walked to the kitchen and picked up a casserole, protecting her hands with two padded mitts. "Like I said to Betsy, the thing to do is to think positively and be pre—" One moment Mom was holding the casserole, and the next it had crashed to the floor, splattering macaroni, tuna, mushrooms and cream sauce over half the dining-room floor.

After ten seconds of complete silence, the room exploded with laughter. Even Mom found it excruciatingly funny that she had been preaching about being prepared at the moment of her obvious carelessness.

"You're lucky I made two casseroles, one without mushrooms," she said.

"I think you'd better let me carry in the second one," said Linda. While Mom wiped up the floor, Linda walked to the kitchen, returned with the casserole and cautiously placed it on the hot pad.

"Bravo, Linda!" Everyone clapped and shouted.

"Stop this nonsense and let's pray," said Mom.

The nonsense obviously wasn't meant to stop. They had no sooner begun the meal when Julie said, "Pass the pepper, please." She gave a shake over her plate and the top flew off, covering her macaroni with a thick layer of black pepper.

"Dorothy, did you do this on purpose?"

Dorothy stared back in astounded innocence, saying nothing.

"Actually, I filled up the pepper shaker," said Mom in a subdued voice. "I was sure I had the top screwed on tight."

"Mother, you may say what you like, but I'm eating in the kitchen," said Dorothy. She promptly picked up her plate and left the room.

Linda and her two friends were so choked up with laughter, they could hardly eat.

"It's not this crazy around here all the time," said Linda, half joking and half apologetic.

"I like it. I think it's fun," said Janet. Then, realizing what that sounded like, she added, "I mean, it's not fun to have casseroles drop, but . . . oh, well, you know what I mean. Let's change the subject. Suzanne, please pass the Jell-o."

She reached out as Suzanne passed her the molded gelatine salad that was resting on a bed of crisp lettuce leaves. "Want some, too, Mona?" she asked at the very moment that the plate was transferred to her hands. It tipped forward and the lettuce leaves slid off, taking the gelatine with them. It separated into two parts, one landing in Janet's lap and the other in Mona's.

"Thanks a lot, Janet," said Mona drily, before the room again was filled with bursts of hilarity.

"Now *I* feel like moving to the kitchen," said Carol, as soon as things had calmed down a little.

"No, I have it," said Linda. "Don't pass any more food to anyone. If you want something, calmly get up and go help yourself; then go back to your chair, keeping your eyes alert. Got that? We may get through this meal yet."

"That's what I've been saying all day," said Betsy. "If you would all stop thinking about Friday the thirteenth and concentrate on what you're doing, nothing would go wrong."

"Well, my bad luck hit this morning, so I'm not too worried anymore," said Sara.

"We've all been hit, and yet it keeps striking again," said Carol.

"That's not true," Betsy disagreed. "Nothing happened to me or Dad or Linda or Suzanne."

"Mmm. I suppose I'd better admit that I had three feedsacks overflow on me when I was grinding at Farmer's Exchange." Dad looked mischievous instead of resentful.

"Would you believe it? I brought the wrong books

home and accidentally left behind all the ones I'm supposed to be studying this weekend," said Linda sheepishly. "I discovered it in the car after we were almost here."

"That was no accident," said Betsy. "You were secretly telling yourself you weren't going to study anyway."

"Only you and Betsy are left, Suzanne. Come on, confess."

"To tell you the truth, I did have something ridiculous happen this morning," acknowledged Suzanne. "I walked out of the dorm wearing one black shoe and one brown one and got halfway to class before I noticed it. I was so embarrassed I nearly fainted."

"Betsy, that leaves only you. Something must have happened, only you're keeping it a secret. Let us in on it," Carol pressed her.

"Absolutely nothing," Betsy assured them, "and nothing will happen, either. I don't believe in such superstitions."

For the rest of the evening the family laughed and joked and recalled other silly things that had occurred during the day. Occasionally, Betsy noticed some of them talking in whispers the moment she stepped back into the room.

"They're trying to trip me up," she thought, but she wasn't annoyed about it. She pretended she noticed nothing but went about her affairs calmly, with both eyes open.

As she undressed and prepared to jump into her bunk bed, Betsy was about to congratulate herself on having made it through the day, when she glanced at her blankets. They looked suspiciously neat and tidy. Cautiously, she pulled out one side that had been tucked in tightly, expecting a fake frog or jumping jack or some other toy to bounce up at her. There was no sign of one.

"They must have done something," she thought. "Perhaps they put it where my feet would touch it." Extending her arm under the bedcovers, she explored tentatively.

"So that's it! They've short-sheeted my bed."

Calmly and methodically, Betsy stripped her bed and made it up again.

"There's nothing to be afraid of on Friday the thirteenth," she thought smugly as she settled herself comfortably for sleep.

A Toy for Toodles

Betsy's lucky days came to an abrupt halt two weekends later, just after they had done their annual sausage-making and meat-smoking. Uncle Fran and his family came to pick up their meat, bringing Bette Ann's new little dog along. It was part terrier, but mostly chihuahua, and so tiny it could fit in one of Dad's hands. When Betsy cradled it in her arms she thought she'd never seen anything so adorable.

"Here, Toodles," called Bette Ann, and the dog jumped out of Betsy's arms.

"Want to see her do tricks?" asked Bette Ann. When Betsy and her sisters nodded and shouted, "Yes!" she called her mother over because Toodles obeyed Aunt

Mickey best of all: she would roll over and play dead, sit up, extend her paw to shake hands, and when Aunt Mickey cried, "Speak, Toodles!" she would give a short bark. But when she was commanded, "Sing, Toodles!" she would let out a long-drawn-out whine that sounded just like a singer's voice sliding down the scale.

"Bring out her bone," said Aunt Mickey, and Bette Ann went to her bag and dug around until she located a pink plastic bone.

"She got this as a baby present from Grandma, when she was a puppy," explained Aunt Mickey. "It's pink because she's a girl dog, and it's her favorite toy."

They watched as Aunt Mickey held up the bone and made Toodles beg for it and speak. Once Toodles had the bone in her mouth she would not let go, even though Aunt Mickey grabbed and pulled hard at one end. Toodles danced and skittered and hung on tight, and when Aunt Mickey lifted the bone high into the air, there was Toodles, dangling and squirming, but hanging on for dear life.

"Will she always stay this small?" asked Betsy. The idea of having a dog you could carry on the end of a bone, or in a small purse, was so appealing she was already half planning to ask for one on her next birthday.

"She's six months old and will grow some more, but not too much," said Aunt Mickey.

Roon and Trixie, their two farm dogs, growled at Toodles when Betsy and Bette Ann took her outside for a short run in the snow. Toodles yapped at them, unafraid. They chased her, but she could outrun them because her lightweight paws did not sink into the snow whereas their big, chunky ones broke through at every step, slowing them down.

"Bring her in," called Aunt Mickey from the back porch. "She's a house dog and it would be too dangerous to leave her out there for long. One of the cows would be sure to step on her."

At night, when the girls went to bed, Bette Ann took Toodles upstairs with her.

"Don't you think she should stay downstairs and sleep in her basket?" asked Aunt Mickey.

"She likes to curl up in my sleeping bag with me," said Bette Ann.

"Yes, let her sleep in our room," pleaded Betsy.

It took them a long time to settle down for the night. The seven girls talked and laughed so loudly, Mom called up from the foot of the steps, "If you don't quiet down I'm not going to let you come and help make doughnuts."

After that, they whispered and giggled softly because they all wanted to go to early Mass and afterward down to the church basement, to assist in the making of the hundreds of doughnuts that were sold after all the Masses. Usually they did the sugaring and frosting, and Mom let them eat as many different doughnuts as they wanted.

"I wonder if Toodles likes doughnuts," whispered Betsy.

"She likes almost anything," answered Bette Ann softly. "Mom calls her our little garbage disposal."

Finally they fell asleep.

A rustling, snuffling noise woke Betsy. In the dim morning light she could see only faint outlines and rough shapes. Peering over the edge of her bunk, she tried to see what was making the strange sounds. A small white figure moved in the far corner.

"Toodles, is that you?" whispered Betsy.

The dog pricked up its ears, looked at her, and then turned back to something on the floor and began chewing on it.

"Have you got your bone?" asked Betsy in her sweetest talking-to-the-dog voice. Toodles did not look up this time.

The hall light went on and Mom called up the stairs, "Time to get up."

Betsy climbed out of her bunk, switched on the overhead light, and turned toward Toodles. Then she gasped in horror. Clasped in Toodles' jaws, and sticking out so it looked as though she had one pink inner lip hanging loose, was Betsy's retainer.

"Bette Ann! Mary! Donna!" shrieked Betsy. "Get up! Quick!" She walked slowly toward the corner where Toodles was standing and staring back at her.

"What's the matter?" asked Bette Ann, sitting up.

"Toodles has my retainer. She thinks it's her bone!" Betsy hoped and prayed that the little dog had not chewed on it too much.

"How did she get it?" Bette Ann leaped out of her

sleeping bag and moved alongside Betsy in the hope they could trap Toodles in the corner.

"She must have climbed into the lower bunk and then reached up to the table. That's where I always put it and I'm sure I did last night, too."

Now Donna, Mary and Julie were also up. As soon as they saw the situation they came to stand next to Betsy and Bette Ann, forming a half-circle.

"Talk to her nice and slow," directed Julie as they moved closer and closer to the dog.

"Here, Toodles," called Bette Ann. "Give me the bone, Toodles."

Toodles thought the girls were in as playful a mood as she was. She dashed past them, running right between Bette Ann's legs, and then turned around and glanced back as if to say, "I fooled you that time, didn't I?"

The commotion had awakened Sara and Kristine, so they joined in the chase. Around and around the room the girls hopped and leaped, but Toodles was too quick for them. She would scoot under the beds or the bureaus and then, before they could completely surround the piece of furniture and seize her as she came out, she would slip through the one spot that wasn't covered by someone's legs or arms. Once, she let go of the retainer and it dropped to the floor.

"Grab it!" shouted Betsy. She was too far away, but Sara and Mary were close.

Mary flopped down on the floor, trying to cover the retainer with her body, but Toodles was faster. She snatched it up and moved away just as Mary's chest hit the rug with a thud.

At last they succeeded in cornering Toodles and Bette Ann grasped her by the body and legs while Mary tried to take the retainer from her jaws. Toodles hung on tight, still thinking it was her bone, and growled softly as she bared her teeth. Betsy could see the sharp canine teeth chomped down firmly on the pink plastic.

"She's probably put a hole right through it" she said unhappily.

"I've got an idea," cried Bette Ann. "Here, hold Toodles a minute." She ran down the stairs and came back a moment later with a dog biscuit.

"Speak, Toodles!" commanded Bette Ann. "Speak!"

At first Toodles merely cocked her head and looked up at them from Mary's lap.

"Set her down so she can sit up and beg," said Bette Ann.

"She'll run away again," complained Betsy.

"No, she won't. She likes these dog biscuits. Sit, Toodles! Sit!"

Mary let go of Toodles and she sat on her haunches, paws extended.

"Speak, Toodles! Speak!"

"Woof!" barked Toodles and the retainer dropped from her jaws. All the girls grabbed for it, but Betsy got it first.

"Good dog!" cried Bette Ann, petting Toodles and giving her the biscuit.

"She steals my retainer and you call her a good dog?" exclaimed Betsy. She no longer thought Toodles was such a cute pet as she examined the retainer and saw two deep dents in the plastic where Toodles' teeth had pressed hard.

Life did not seem fair to Betsy. She had carefully put the retainer in a safe place, only to discover that with Toodles around, no place was really safe.

"That old superstition isn't true," she thought. "Disasters don't come in threes, they keep on coming forever."

She wasn't even relieved when Dr. Shayner told her, on the following Monday, that she had needed a new retainer anyway so it didn't matter what damage Toodles had done. Then Dr. Shayner told Betsy something else that made her realize she would have to be more vigilant than ever.

"Your teeth are just about where they should be, so this will probably be the last mold we'll make. We'll give you a smaller retainer, but you'll have to keep wearing it for a few years more, I believe, to make sure your teeth stay in the same position.

"A few years!" groaned Betsy. She had been wearing a retainer for slightly less than a year and look at all the accidents that had happened! How was she ever going to keep it safe during all that time?

"Be grateful you don't have to wear metal braces," said Dr. Shayner. "They often have to stay on for years and years, and they're much more expensive."

"Yes," Betsy felt like telling him, "but at least they stay in your mouth all the time." However, she kept silent.

She was so glum when she came home from the dentist the following Saturday with her new retainer, that to cheer herself up she decided to make another ice lady in her bottle, since the weather had turned cold again. But after experimenting with both the lady bottle and her fish bottle, and finding out it was not quite cold enough to freeze quickly, she put them away in disgust. Nothing was working out right. She felt as though somewhere on her body was a pimple about to break out, but she did not know where to scratch.

Clogs into Space

Betsy's irritable, dissatisfied mood came to a head in March, and the person who pinched the pimple of bad feeling in her was Julie. The first squeeze occurred at a rummage sale held in their church.

"Here's five dollars for each of you," said Mom. "You may buy anything you like."

Julie and Dorothy ran off as though they knew exactly what they wanted, but Betsy, Sara and Kristine looked around and hesitated, wondering in which direction they should move first.

The church basement was crowded with tables and each of them was covered with a jumble of secondhand articles. There were tables piled high with pots and pans, dishes, glassware, knickknacks and jewelry. Other tables had baskets, plants, pillows, lamps, pictures and books. Beyond them were tables with mounds of clothing separated into categories: blouses, sweaters, shirts, dresses, pants, pajamas, nightgowns, slips and underwear. Only the jackets and coats and suits were hung up on racks. In the back, behind the clothing, was a space where small pieces of furniture were displayed.

Betsy moved slowly from table to table, looking closely to see if she might come upon some treasure she wanted. She was interrupted in her slow progress by Julie.

"Look what I found for exactly five dollars!" Julie held out a pair of almost-new clogs. In fact, they were so new they hardly looked worn, and they were the expensive kind. "They fit me to a *T*," she added.

A wave of jealousy engulfed Betsy. She could hardly bring herself to speak, and then it was only in an effort to negate Julie's good luck.

"Mom won't let you keep them," she said.

"Oh yes she will. She said we could buy anything we wanted. That's why I went looking for them right off. I knew she'd never buy us any new ones, but at a rummage sale she doesn't care what we get." Julie had obviously wanted clogs as much as Betsy.

Mom wasn't too happy about it but she gave in, reluctantly acknowledging she could not go back on her word.

"I should have said, 'Buy anything *except* clogs,'" she admitted ruefully.

"Let me try them on, Julie," pleaded Betsy.

"Okay." Julie was glowing with goodwill.

The clogs were only a bit too large for Betsy. She was sure that if she wore thick socks, they would fit her nicely.

"I'll let you wear them to school someday," Julie continued in her generosity. "But don't you dare take them out of our closet without asking me first."

For more than a week, Julie wore her clogs to school every day, and each morning Betsy felt the ache of envy deepen. One Thursday morning, they woke to a freak snowstorm, and Mom insisted they all wear boots over their shoes, so Julie had to leave her clogs in the closet, for no boots fit over their bulkiness.

"But I'm going to Grandma's house tonight. I have my flute lesson. That means I can't wear them for two days in a row," she protested.

"Too bad," said Mom, "but you're not wearing them in this weather. I don't want you twisting an ankle or falling and breaking a leg."

That evening, Betsy asked her mother to listen to her as she ran through a dress rehearsal of her part in a pageant they were having in school on Friday. It was called "Hello, World," and her class was to present it to the first three grades. Each fourth grader would wear a costume from a different country and tell about special things that came from the country or that had happened there. Betsy was sure hers was going to be one of the best presentations because she had an authentic costume from Afghanistan that Aunt Anne had given her, and she had studied up on the country until she knew so much about it, she almost felt she had been there.

She slipped on the yellow pantaloons and over them the maroon dress with its tiny mirrors in the bodice, outlined in beautiful embroidery stitched in gold threads.

Around the skirt were sewn two rows of shiny metal coins that clinked and tinkled like tiny bells whenever she moved.

As soon as she was dressed in her costume, Betsy had a brilliant idea. Why hadn't she thought of it before?

"Julie's clogs! They would be perfect to wear with this outfit."

"I'm not so sure about that," said Mom. "If you were going as a little Dutch girl they'd look fine, but with that costume they might look out of place."

"Now you admit they still wear them in Holland," retorted Betsy. "Well, I think they wear something like clogs in Afghanistan, too. The toes are a bit more pointy, maybe, but they look like clogs." Betsy ran to get one of the library books she had on Afghanistan, to show Mom a picture.

"But Julie won't like it if you wear them without her permission," argued Mom.

"I'll call her," said Betsy, and immediately she ran to the telephone and dialed Grandma's number.

"Julie isn't here," said Grandma. "Kathy took her to a swim show at the college. They won't be back until ten or so."

"Grandma, would you please ask her to call me when she comes in?"

"Grandpa and I will be in bed by then," said Grandma.

Betsy knew that meant Julie wouldn't be allowed to make any calls so late.

"Will you leave her a note that I want to wear her clogs with my Afghanistan costume for the pageant tomorrow? Tell her to call me in the morning if it's not okay."

"That I can do," said Grandma.

131

In the morning Betsy packed her costume in a bag and then searched in the clothes basket on the back porch for the thickest pair of wool socks she could find. Yesterday's storm had petered out quickly and the snow was gone, so she did not have to wear boots. There was no call from Julie, which meant Betsy had permission to wear the clogs.

"Everything is working out perfectly," thought Betsy as she thonked out to the car.

The pageant was to take place first thing in the morning. After prayers, Miss Lanzoni let the girls go into the cloakroom to change while the boys put on their costumes at their desks.

"Oh, how funny," giggled Christie as she saw the yellow pantaloons. But when Betsy slipped on the tinkling dress, Christie and all the girls "Oh'd" and "Ah'd."

"You're beautiful, Betsy," said Christie as she and another friend helped arrange the blue veil over Betsy's head.

"Thank you," said Betsy, smiling broadly, no longer afraid to show her teeth.

The pupils in Grade Four took at least fifteen minutes to settle down as they admired each other's costume or whooped and stomped in silly, exaggerated gestures, getting rid of any embarrassment they might have about wearing the different clothes. At last they were ready to file into the auditorium, filling the rows at one side, where the steps led up to the stage. In the center rows sat the first, second and third graders, trying hard not to wiggle and squirm.

"They're learning how to sit properly for a program in a theater," thought Betsy, remembering Mrs. Koller's

and Miss Brandt's helpful instructions from second and third grade.

The lights dimmed, the piano announced the beginning of the pageant, and Betsy shut her eyes and ears, concentrating only on her part and the words she must speak. From their practice sessions, she had learned that she dared not listen too closely to the classmates who spoke their parts before her, because she would end up memorizing their words and forgetting hers.

"I come from Afghanistan, an ancient Asian land of high mountains and fertile, green valleys. . . ." Over and over Betsy silently mouthed her speech until Miss Lanzoni gave her a gentle nudge and it was her turn.

Feeling nervous and tense she walked up the steps and crossed to the middle of the stage; the clinking of the coins made a pleasant Christmasy sound that gave her more confidence with each step she took. When she turned to face the audience, she could see that the children weren't pointing and giggling as they had at some of the other performers. They were quiet and almost unmoving, as though awestruck.

"I come from Afghanistan . . ." began Betsy, taking a deep breath and speaking loudly and clearly, as Miss Lanzoni had requested. She finished her piece and the audience applauded.

"It's over," thought Betsy, relaxing with relief. But it wasn't over at all.

Walking toward the steps, she didn't realize that she had never practiced going down stairs while wearing the clogs, and that she must curl her toes tightly to hold on to them.

In the split second of actually taking the first step, she recognized the danger, and tried to hold on to the clog, but her thick sock prevented her toes from gripping the slippery wood.

Off into space went the clog, hurtling toward her classmates. They all ducked, but the clog landed with a thunk on someone's head and then clattered to the floor.

Betsy stood at the top step, struck with horror. The piano continued playing, but she couldn't bring herself to move. One of the mothers who had been watching came forward to help, and Miss Lanzoni came to the foot of the steps and called out to Betsy in a terse voice.

"Come and take your seat."

Filled with shame, Betsy hobbled down the steps. The thonk of one clog did not sound satisfying—it sounded dreadful. She sat down feeling miserable.

"Here's your other shoe," whispered a classmate, passing the other clog to Betsy.

"Next!" hissed Miss Lanzoni. "Keep moving." Then she whispered to the mother, "Take him to the nurse and have her put ice on it."

Betsy could see now that it was Joey who had been hit by her clog, because a lump was already starting to appear on his upper forehead, where his hair had been pushed aside.

There had been a flurry of excited gasps and whispers after the clog episode, but the audience soon calmed down. Betsy slumped in her seat, sunk in misery. At the end of the pageant she walked with the rest of her class back to the fourth-grade room. She was afraid they would taunt her or tease her, but instead they remained subdued and sympathetically silent for the rest of the morning. Even Miss Lanzoni did not reproach her.

"It could have happened to any of us," said Christie, trying to console Betsy.

But that afternoon Julie wasn't as calm about it.

"You had no right to wear my clogs," she scolded.

"Didn't Grandma leave you a note? She said she would and you didn't call in the morning."

"I did, too," Julie contradicted. "I didn't see the note right away and by the time I called, you had left."

Now Betsy felt even worse, to think she had worn the clogs without Julie's permission. Mom was a great believer in the personal- and private-property system. Each one had her own things and they were supposed to share but only if and when they felt generous, and never, ever were they supposed to use another's possessions without asking. Betsy liked the system and recognized that she would have been as upset as Julie.

"Actually, I was going to tell you that you could wear them," said Julie as she noticed Betsy's distress.

That made Betsy feel a little better, but the same heavy depression descended on her again on Monday when they learned that in all the lower grades, clogs were forbidden for the duration.

"Everything is against me," thought Betsy.

Goodbye, Grandpa

That March and April, which coincided with Lent, was the most trying time Betsy had ever experienced. The girls at school were annoyed that they could no longer wear clogs.

"You would have to spoil it for all of us," said Julie.

"It was an accident," said Betsy. She didn't think it was fair of Julie to keep rubbing it in. She felt bad enough without her accusing looks and words.

"I don't even feel like giving up anything for Lent," said Betsy to herself. It seemed enough of a sacrifice to forget about any chance of wearing the clogs, because after school and on weekends Julie always wore them. But instead of making her feel like a better person, as she had always felt when giving up candy in earlier years, Betsy responded to the clogless days with petulance and bad temper.

When Mom or Dad called, she often pretended not to hear. She yelled at Danny for no good reason except that he always seemed to be ready to tease her. With Dorothy, Julie, and Mona she argued violently and frequently over whose turn it was to do the dishes in the evening, and often they gave in, even when it was her turn, because she was so unpleasant about it. And she stubbornly refused to play with Sara and Kristine whenever they asked, even though there were times she really would have liked to join in with their pretend games. It was as though the spring rains, instead of bringing budding flowers and sprouting plants, carried only a cold anger that seeped up from the damp ground like an odorless gas that made one sick.

By the time Holy Week arrived, Betsy was certain no one would ever forgive her. On Good Friday the family went to church and she sat in the pew, pondering her shortcomings. The quiet church, with its ghostly, purple-draped figures, seemed exactly right for examining her conscience. When she came out of the confessional she prayed earnestly.

"I'll obey my parents right away, the moment they call me, and I'll try not to get angry at my brother and sisters," she promised. "And I'm really, truly happy that Julie found the clogs first, because then she can wear them for a while and pass them on to me, and if I take care of them they'll still be good for Sara. That way three of us get to wear them." Betsy was convinced she had swept envy and jealousy from her heart.

She got an opportunity to test her new resolution to

behave better the moment they returned home. Kathy called from Grandma's house with the saddest, most mournful news: Grandpa had had another heart attack that afternoon, and this time he had died.

"At least I wasn't fooling around or getting mad at somebody," thought Betsy. It was comforting to think she had been praying for her family and herself at the moment of Grandpa's death.

The days that followed were a blur of telephone calls, drives to the airport to pick up the aunts, evening prayers at the mortuary, baking and cooking to take care of all the company, and endless dishwashing. Fortunately Linda was home from college and could take charge because Mom spent every day in town with Grandma, trying to console her.

The cousins arrived and stayed at the farm and so did Uncle Ed and Aunt Mary. On Saturday evening they colored dozens of eggs, and every now and then Betsy or one of her sisters or cousins would burst into laughter at the funny way some of the designs and colors turned out. Then they would think of Grandpa and settle down quickly and be sober again. Such an aura of goodwill and cooperativeness reigned that it was almost too much for Betsy to bear, after weeks of wrangling and bickering.

"Does this mean we can't behave ourselves unless someone dies?" she wondered.

For Easter Mass they went to St. Stanislaus Church with Grandma instead of going to the cathedral as they usually did. It was hard for Grandma to be in church for the first Easter without Grandpa, and tears coursed down her cheeks, dripping on the new silk dress Grandpa had bought her. The salty tears made stains of deep violet against the pale lilac silk, and Grandma tried to blot them up with her handkerchief.

"Maybe she's worried no one will buy her clothes and food and things," thought Betsy, and she leaned over and squeezed Grandma's hand.

"Don't worry, Grandma, we'll take care of you," whispered Betsy.

The funeral was on Monday and the children stood back as Mom and Uncle Fran and the aunts solicitously held on to Grandma in turns. She sobbed and sobbed as the coffin was rolled away and the choir sang sad songs in Polish.

"Goodbye, Grandpa," said Betsy silently, after the priest had intoned the final "May he rest in peace" and everyone answered "Amen."

Grandma's house was crowded for the dinner following the funeral. Grandpa's sister, Aunt Emeline, and his two brothers, Uncle Felix and Uncle Martin, came with some of their children and grandchildren. And Grandma's brothers were there, too: Uncle Roman, Uncle Leo and Uncle August. There were first cousins and second cousins and, of course, Great-great Aunt Pauline. Names were called out and Betsy tried to remember the faces to match them later: Aunt Amelia, Aunt Arvilla, Aunt Helen, Aunt Mera, Uncle Frank, Imelda, Sally Ann, Anthony, Mabel, Suzanne, Bernice, Mary Ann, Eddie, Margaret, Jim, Fay, Betty Lou, Laura, Greg, Eleanore, Andy, Dorothy, Celia, Basil, Clarence, Delores, Joe, Bernell, Richard, Melvin, Harold, David, Nancy, Vic, Virgil—there seemed no end to them, and Betsy gave up attempting to keep them straight.

Sitting at the table crowded with plates and platters

and bowls of good things to eat reminded her of something.

"This is like the reunion we had."

Grandma began to cry again when she heard that, and Betsy felt sorry she had said anything.

"You're right, Betsy," said Aunt Janie, "and I think Dad would want it to be just as happy and full of fun. Let's have a song fest this afternoon. Virgie, you have to lead us in the orchestra song."

When the tables were cleared away, Aunt Virgie divided them up into groups and reviewed the sounds of the instruments. Grandma still shed a few tears, but mostly she laughed at the sounds the singers made as they acted out the instruments.

"I want to be a *maududel*," said Betsy, switching from one group to the next. She loved the silly sound of that instrument, even though no one knew quite what it was.

"Doo doo, doo doo, doo doo, doo doo," hooted the *maududel*s as the trumpet singers brassily trumpeted, "Tara, tara, tara, ta ta." The bass fiddlers harumphed their way through "Oom-pah, oom-pah, oom-pah-pah."

They sang and sang until they could think of no more songs.

"It's so nice out; let's do some square dancing in the front yard," suggested Kathy.

There were enough persons to make several circles, and after reviewing the basic steps Kathy led them through a simple dance.

"Oh, dear," thought Betsy as she was being swung wildly by one of her cousins. "Grandpa loved to dance, but he didn't think it was right to do it during Lent. I wonder if he would be upset that we're dancing on his funeral day." She couldn't hold the thought very long because she was caught up in the swinging rhythms and the intricate weaving in and out. She passed Aunt Janie, twirling and twisting around and around in the circle.

"Why, she likes dancing as much as I do," thought Betsy.

Grandma came out on the front porch.

"Jane, people are going to think we're crazy," said Grandma.

"Don't worry, Mom. If they stop to stare or comment we'll just say we're dancing Grandpa right into heaven," said Aunt Janie as she continued dancing.

Grandma smiled and shook her head and then went back inside.

"If Aunt Janie thinks it's all right to dance at Grandpa's funeral, then it must be," decided Betsy, and although she gave up her body to the dancing her thoughts remained with Grandpa.

Sibling Rivalry Again

Because it was Easter Week there was no school after Grandpa's funeral, and the cousins stayed on at the farm. Every day a few of the children were scheduled to go to Grandma's house to be with her and to run errands if she or the aunts needed anything.

"I'm staying here on the farm," announced Rob on Tuesday. "Uncle Roman says Hattie is about to have her calf any hour now, and I want to be here when she does."

"Me, too," said Mike.

"I want to see it, too," said Donna.

"And I do, too," added Mary.

Mom took Betsy aside and asked her a favor: "Would

you be sure to go off and play somewhere with Donna and Mary and Sara and Kristine when Hattie is ready to have her calf?"

"Why?" asked Betsy. "They want to watch."

"I know," said Mom. "But Uncle Fran and Aunt Mickey think Donna and Mary are too little. They want to wait awhile yet."

"But Sara and Kristine are the same ages and they've seen calves born," replied Betsy.

"They're used to it," explained Mom. "But Donna and Mary may be frightened."

"They'll be mad if they can't watch," protested Betsy. "I don't think there's anything to be afraid of."

"Betsy, try to remember the first time you saw a calf born," insisted Mom. "Weren't you a little queasy about all the blood and the messy wetness of the newborn calf? It was only later that you looked happy about it, when you could see that the calf looked fine and strong and glossy. I'm not sure Donna and Mary will be around long enough to see that, so they might end up being upset. Now will you please cooperate and take them off somewhere when Dad or I give you the signal?"

"Okay," agreed Betsy, but she was still not convinced it was necessary.

That evening, after supper, Dad put on his coat again instead of settling down with the evening paper.

"I want to check on those steers in the pole barn," he said. "Rob and Mike, do you want to come along?"

"I'll go, Uncle Roman," offered Donna.

"It's kind of dark out there," said Dad, "and you have on your good clothes and shoes. You'd better stay here."

"I'll change. Sara will give me something old, won't you, Sara?"

"Betsy, I thought you said you were going to start a game of Chinese checkers," said Mom, nudging Betsy.

"Heavens to me!" thought Betsy. "The signal. Mom must be asking me to take them off to play."

"Donna, you promised you'd play a game after supper. We need you to fill up the points of the star: you and Sara, Teensie and Mary, Julie and me." Betsy was sure Donna would see the reasoning behind her argument because Dave and John and Bette Ann, the other three cousins, were in town at Grandma's.

"All right," said Donna, giving in. She really wanted to go out to the barn but, like the others, was still trying to be on her best behavior.

The six girls settled themselves happily around the low table, fitted the colored marbles into the appropriate slots, and began their game. A pleasant sensation of duty fulfilled passed through Betsy as she moved the smooth marbles along their paths. She hoped her parents were pleased at the ease with which she had distracted Donna and Mary.

The first game ended and they began another, switching colors and partners so that Betsy and Julie, who had won the first round, were no longer playing opposite each other. When the second game was over, Donna didn't want to start a third.

"What's keeping them so long in the barn?" she asked. "Can I go and see, Aunt Angie?"

Betsy looked at her mother, wondering how she would answer, but Mom didn't have to reply because at that moment Rob and Mike returned with Dad.

"That was fantastic!" said Rob. "The way those tiny hoofs push out and then the head and then all the rest."

"You mean to tell me Hattie had her calf and you

144

didn't call me?" wailed Donna. "You knew I wanted to watch."

"You're too little for that," said Rob, with so much scorn in his voice that it even made Betsy wince.

"Don't rub it in like that," she told him as Donna stared at the two of them.

"Betsy, you knew where they were going! You traitor! Why didn't you tell us?"

Betsy looked helplessly at her mother, but Mom said nothing, and Betsy suspected she was also not supposed to say that it was Donna's parents who hadn't wanted her to see the calf born.

"So much for you!" Donna spat out the words in Betsy's face. "I'm never going to play with you again." She linked arms with Sara.

"That was mean, Betsy. Why did you do it?" asked Sara, taking sides with Donna.

"Don't get so mad. We can go and watch another time," said Mary.

"Then play with her yourself if you want to. I think she's sneaky and I don't want to have any friends like that." With a flip of her red ponytails, Donna turned her back on them and walked away, pulling Sara with her.

"It's not fair," thought Betsy. "I do something as a favor to Uncle Fran and Aunt Mickey, and yet I get in trouble."

There was bigger trouble ahead, because on Wednesday Grandma particularly asked to have Betsy, Sara and Donna come and spend the day with her.

"Mom, I don't want to go with them. Can't I go tomorrow with Mary and Kristine?" pleaded Betsy.

"We don't want to go with you any more than you want to go with us," taunted Sara.

"I'll go, but I'm not playing with her," said Donna, refusing to even mention Betsy's name.

"Girls, I will not have this quarreling," said Mom in her no-nonsense voice. "Donna, if you're still so upset about not seeing the calf born, you'll have to take it up with your parents because it was they who didn't want you to. Now get in the car and let's not hear another word about it."

Wearing stubborn, sullen looks, the three girls climbed into the car: Betsy in the front seat by her mother, and Sara and Donna in the back.

"I'll be glad not to say another word to them," thought Betsy.

"Here are my three girlies!" cried Grandma happily. "I asked for you three because I felt in the mood to do some sewing to get my mind off things. I had this dress started and I'm not quite sure which one of you it will fit best." She brought out a cotton print of white-and-yellow daisies on a green background.

First Sara tried it on and then Donna and, last of all, Betsy. It was too long-waisted for Sara, but not for Donna and Betsy.

"Dear me! It fits you both. Donna, you're nearly as tall as Betsy," exclaimed Grandma. "Aren't you almost two years apart?"

"A year and a half." Donna said stiffly.

"You can give the dress to Donna," said Betsy, determined to show Grandma her best side.

"That's okay," said Donna, glancing at her mother. "If Betsy wants it, she can have it."

"Such nice, unselfish grandchildren I have," said Grandma, giving each of them a squeeze. "I think, if you don't mind, Betsy, I'll give the dress to Donna. I don't get to sew as much for her."

Betsy blushed with embarrassment as she mumbled, "That's just fine, Grandma." She felt ashamed because her offer had been made out of politeness, not out of generosity. She kept her eyes averted from her mother's face.

The three girls were quiet and polite for the rest of the morning, sitting and listening to the grown-ups instead of playing with each other. Betsy noticed that Donna did not say a word to her parents about missing the birth of the calf. After dinner Mom and Uncle Fran and Aunt Mickey went out to take care of some business, and Grandma settled down to a game of bridge with Aunt Millie, Aunt Mary and Uncle Ed.

Betsy selected a book from Grandma's bookcase and sat on the sofa, pretending to read intently. Sara and Donna spread out their coloring books on the dining-room table and took out the giant box of crayons Grandma kept in a desk drawer. Betsy loved to use those crayons because they were sharper than hers at home and all of the colors were still there; but she was not about to ask if she could share one of Donna's or Sara's pages, and they certainly didn't seem to be ready to offer it on their own.

During a break in the bridge game, Aunt Millie went to the kitchen to check on the food.

"We have enough casseroles and vegetables to heat up for supper, but I sure would love to have some more *kielbasa*," she sighed.

"I think Angie brought the last of what she had," said Aunt Mary.

"You could always get some from Tushner's," suggested Grandma. "Their sausages are almost as good as homemade."

"I'll go and buy some," offered Betsy. She had been listening to the conversation in the hope it would offer something more interesting to do.

"That's a good idea," said Aunt Millie, reaching for her purse. "You three girls can walk to Tushner's. You know the way, don't you?"

Betsy nodded, though she would have preferred going alone.

"Here's enough to buy at least four rings, and a treat for yourselves." Aunt Millie handed Betsy several bills.

"Better take it in a little purse," said Grandma. Betsy almost answered back that she was old enough to know how to take care of money, but she caught herself in time.

"Sara! Donna! I've given Betsy money for a treat. Go with her to Tushner's and help carry home the *kielbasa*." Aunt Millie gave the instructions as though they were orders, and the two girls obeyed without a peep of protest.

Once outside, however, they berated Betsy with bitter words.

"We don't want to go *anywhere* with *you!*"

"We wouldn't have come if Aunt Millie hadn't said anything."

"Well, don't come and see if I care!" said Betsy as, angry and hurt, she walked down to the end of the block and turned up Hamilton Street in the direction of Tushner's. Sara and Donna continued following her, but she could hear them discussing other plans.

"Let's go to Dirty Park while she's at Tushner's," said Donna. "It's not too far away from here, is it?"

Dirty Park was a small park nearby, and the children called it by that name because whenever they came home from playing there, the grownups would always say, "I don't know how you can get so dirty playing in that park!"

"It's pretty close," answered Sara. "But what about our treats?"

"She can get the change and give it to us and we'll buy our treats at the store near Grandma's," said Donna.

"Okay." Sara sounded hesitant, but she gave in to her cousin.

"We're not going with you to Tushner's," Donna called to Betsy. "We're going to Dirty Park."

Betsy didn't even reply, she was so humiliated. She marched forward in the direction of Third Street and didn't look back until she had gone two blocks. In the distance she could still see Sara and Donna, walking arm in arm in the direction opposite to her.

"Why are they going that way?" she asked aloud. "They should have turned right on Seventh Street. Doesn't that silly Sara know the way?" A niggling worry wormed up inside her. What if they got lost?

Betsy entered Tushner's and forgot her concern while she waited her turn at the counter, smelling the same meaty, smoky odors that surrounded their smokehouse. She purchased the *kielbasa* and a package of Cracker Jacks.

The uneasiness hit her again as she started back to Grandma's house, and it grew deeper as she came to Seventh Street.

"I suppose I'd better go and see what they're up to in Dirty Park," she sighed. But Sara and Donna were up to nothing, for there was not a sign of them anywhere in the small park.

"They probably decided to go back to Grandma's," Betsy told herself. But for some reason the hollow feeling in the pit of her stomach wouldn't go away.

She had reason to be worried because Sara and Donna were not at Grandma's house, either.

"Where are Sara and Donna?" asked Grandma.

"They wanted to play in Dirty Park," said Betsy, avoiding the fact that she had been to the park and had not seen them. She wanted to tell someone about it, but not Grandma.

When Aunt Millie paused in the game and went to the kitchen for a moment, Betsy mentioned it to her.

"They were probably hiding from you," said Aunt Millie.

Betsy sat down with relief. If Aunt Millie didn't see

any reason to worry, neither should she. Yet when Mom and Uncle Fran and Aunt Mickey came back, she again expressed her concern.

"Sara should know the way to the park," Mom agreed.

"We still have some business to take care of," said Aunt Mickey. "We'll drive by there and check up on them."

They were back in ten minutes, looking more distressed than Betsy, but they waited until they were in the kitchen before speaking.

"There isn't a sign of them around the park, and we checked the streets for quite a few blocks. Betsy, where did you say you last saw them?" Uncle Fran spoke low so Grandma couldn't hear.

Betsy described what she had seen. "They were walking in the direction of the lake."

"Let's each take a car and cruise separate streets," said Mom. "One of us is sure to come upon them."

"I'll borrow Ed's car and then all three of us can go," said Aunt Mickey. They heard her in the living room as she nonchalantly asked for permission, "Ed, we still have so many errands to run it sure would be a help if I could use your car."

"Quick, somebody! Write out another insurance policy," joked Uncle Ed as he handed over the keys.

"We'll be back as soon as we find them," said Mom quietly to Betsy. "Should anyone call, have Aunt Millie talk to them, and above all, don't mention it to Grandma. She has enough to be upset about."

Nervously, Betsy paced from the front room to the kitchen and then back again. Occasionally, she would step out on to the front porch and peer down the street. Why weren't they coming? Surely nothing could have happened to Sara and Donna in broad daylight.

"Any sign?" asked Aunt Mickey, coming back a half-hour later.

Betsy shook her head.

"They weren't on any of the streets I covered," said Mom when she returned ten minutes after Aunt Mickey. A cool breeze blew in before she closed the door and all three of them shivered. Betsy felt numb on the outside of her skin, like when she had novocaine at the dentist. But inside she felt prickles of pain, thinking of the terrible things she sometimes heard on the television news: children who were lured off to the woods by strangers and then beaten to death; or, worse yet, who disappeared and were never heard from again.

"Dear God," she prayed, "please bring back Sara and Donna, and I'll always try to be nice to them."

The answer to her prayer came almost immediately, in the form of loud sobbing from the front yard.

"That's Donna. I can tell already," laughed Aunt Mickey nervously as she and Betsy and Mom tried to rush through the door at the same time.

The two girls were both convulsed with sobs, and each headed for her own mother's comforting arms.

"I found them down by the railroad tracks," said Uncle Fran.

Aunt Mickey wrung out a washcloth and gently washed first Donna's and then Sara's face, wiping away the tear streaks. In spite of the prayer she had said no more than a few minutes ago, Betsy felt a pang of jealousy. She hadn't been lost, but she had been dreadfully worried, and no one sought to comfort her.

"We have to get moving on home," said Mom as the two girls at last were calm and quiet.

"I'm staying here," said Donna. There was no way she could be convinced to leave her parents.

In the car, Betsy took out her box of Cracker Jacks and offered some to Sara, but Sara only shook her head, turned her shoulder to Betsy, and snuggled closer to Mom.

"Why is she still mad at me?" asked Betsy in despair. When they got home she felt more resentful than ever, because Sara allowed Kristine and Mary to hug her and pet her while she told them how she got all turned around and ended up at the railroad tracks instead of at the park.

Betsy thought of her mother and her aunts and Uncle Fran and the tender, loving way they had treated Grandma and each other during the past few days.

"I want to be a loving sister, but no one will let me," she thought despondently. "Every time I promise to do better, something happens and I get an attack of sibling rivalry." She remembered how she had first read about sibling rivalry in Linda's book. What was it the author had written? She tried to recall the paragraph and suddenly realized that that was all she had read—one paragraph. What if the book had a lot more to say on the subject? Maybe there was even some advice on how to fight off attacks. Betsy ran to find her oldest sister.

"Linda, do you still have that book from last year—the one with the sibling rivalry in it?"

"You mean my child-development text? It's in my bookcase in my room. Why?"

"I want to look at it right now. It's important."

"I suppose I'd better get it because if I don't you'll go rummaging in my things," Linda complained as she went up to her room, with Betsy following.

"How can I find the part you were using when you observed Sara and Kristine?" asked Betsy as soon as Linda had located the textbook.

Mystified, Linda checked the index and then flipped the book open to the exact page Betsy remembered. The yellow underlining leaped up at her as she scanned the text. At the end of the section were two long paragraphs with the heading "Negative Effects" and "Positive Effects."

"I know all about the negative effects," said Betsy to herself as she allowed her eyes to slip down to the "Positive Effects" part.

In every large family, friction between siblings is common and its positive effects can sometimes outweigh the negative ones. Mild teasing, arguing or quarreling, if it is not the result of parents playing favorites and does not resort to name calling or physical abuse, can often be a healthy means of getting rid of aggression. Or it can be a method of learning to accommodate and get along with different personalities, a skill that is likely to be needed when the children are adults.

Betsy read the paragraph over twice, not sure she understood it exactly the first time.

"What's the matter? Are you worried about something?" asked Linda.

"Never mind," said Betsy. "I have to go and ask Mom something." She slammed shut the textbook and left the room in a hurry.

"I'm the one who studied the book," called Linda, irked that Betsy wasn't consulting her. But Betsy had already clattered down the steps and was on her way to the barn where Mom was doing the milking.

The barn was a perfect place to think through a difficult problem, or to ask for calm advice. The placid cows munching on the hay and the milking machines gently sucking at the cows' udders made soft unhurried noises that seemed to say, "Slow down! No need to rush."

From the hayloft above came the sound of Mona directing Mike, Rob and John as they prepared to toss hay bales close to the chute leading down into the barn. In the stanchions on the far side of the barn, Dorothy was washing the cows' udders.

Betsy watched as her mother sat down on a small

stool, leaned her cheek against Kringle's sleek, rounded belly and then hand-stripped the last remaining milk into the bucket.

"They say twins feel special about each other," Betsy thought as she placed her head next to her mother's. From deep inside Kringle's stomachs she could hear rumblings and gurglings. "I wonder if Kringle misses her twin," she said softly, remembering the day two years ago when they had had a funeral for Kriss, Kringle's twin. Then she thought of all the cows that were like sisters, because they had the same mother. "Do they get jealous of each other?" she wondered, and then smiled because she recalled times when they did seem to get mad at each other, butting and kicking for no apparent reason. Still, cows were not humans and she didn't believe that by observing them she would resolve the questions she had about her own family.

"Mom, did you always get along with Uncle Fran and Aunt Anne and Aunt Millie and all your other sisters when you were little?"

"Betsy, you ask the most unexpected questions," said Mom as she slipped the milking machine deftly from Kringle to the next cow. "And I have a strong suspicion I shouldn't answer this one on the grounds it might incriminate me."

"Please, Mom, tell me the truth." Betsy wasn't in the mood for teasing.

"Well, if you must know, we fought like cats and dogs sometimes."

"I knew it! That's just like the book said. You have to fight when you're little, but you're friends when you grow up."

"Whoa! Wait a minute! Nobody said anything about *having* to fight," laughed Mom, and then she paused. "But I guess we did get most of it out of our systems when we were young."

"Then why do you always scold us kids when we argue?"

Mom thought for a while before she answered.

"I suppose I'm always hoping you won't make the same mistakes we did—quarreling for nothing."

"It's not for nothing," said Betsy. "We're getting used to different personalities."

"Oh, is that so?" asked Mom. "And where did you pick up that idea?"

"From one of Linda's books," answered Betsy.

"Well, if that's the case, then I guess you should have a head start because that's exactly what we have in this family—a dozen different personalities.

"Why, yes!" thought Betsy. "If what the book says is true, I'll be way ahead of most people. I hate it when we bicker and argue so much, but just think of all the friends I'll have when I'm grown up." She smoothed Kringle's furry skin under her cheek and then gave the cow a pat before skipping off to the door.

"Are you going up to do the hay bales with Mona and the boys?" called Mom.

"Not tonight," answered Betsy. "I want to find Julie and try my personality on her." She was sure she would get to wear those clogs again, very soon, and this time she would know how to keep them on her feet.

Family Tree

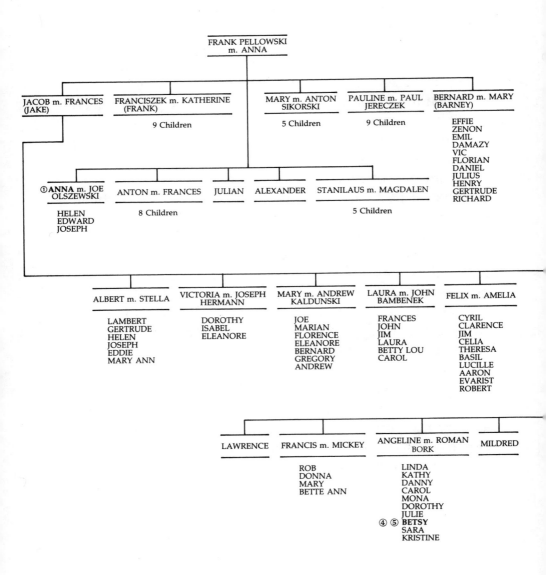

FRANK PELLOWSKI
m. ANNA

JACOB m. FRANCES
(JAKE)

FRANCISZEK m. KATHERINE
(FRANK)
9 Children

MARY m. ANTON
SIKORSKI
5 Children

PAULINE m. PAUL
JERECZEK
9 Children

BERNARD m. MARY
(BARNEY)
EFFIE
ZENON
EMIL
DAMAZY
VIC
FLORIAN
DANIEL
JULIUS
HENRY
GERTRUDE
RICHARD

①**ANNA** m. JOE
OLSZEWSKI
HELEN
EDWARD
JOSEPH

ANTON m. FRANCES
8 Children

JULIAN

ALEXANDER

STANILAUS m. MAGDALEN
5 Children

ALBERT m. STELLA
LAMBERT
GERTRUDE
HELEN
JOSEPH
EDDIE
MARY ANN

VICTORIA m. JOSEPH
HERMANN
DOROTHY
ISABEL
ELEANORE

MARY m. ANDREW
KALDUNSKI
JOE
MARIAN
FLORENCE
ELEANORE
BERNARD
GREGORY
ANDREW

LAURA m. JOHN
BAMBENEK
FRANCES
JOHN
JIM
LAURA
BETTY LOU
CAROL

FELIX m. AMELIA
CYRIL
CLARENCE
JIM
CELIA
THERESA
BASIL
LUCILLE
AARON
EVARIST
ROBERT

LAWRENCE

FRANCIS m. MICKEY
ROB
DONNA
MARY
BETTE ANN

ANGELINE m. ROMAN
BORK
LINDA
KATHY
DANNY
CAROL
MONA
DOROTHY
JULIE
④ ⑤ **BETSY**
SARA
KRISTINE

MILDRED

158

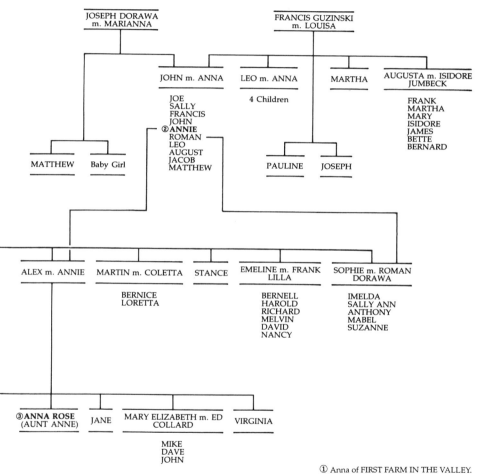

JOSEPH DORAWA
m. MARIANNA

FRANCIS GUZINSKI
m. LOUISA

JOHN m. ANNA

JOE
SALLY
FRANCIS
JOHN
②ANNIE
ROMAN
LEO
AUGUST
JACOB
MATTHEW

LEO m. ANNA

4 Children

MARTHA

AUGUSTA m. ISIDORE
JUMBECK

FRANK
MARTHA
MARY
ISIDORE
JAMES
BETTE
BERNARD

MATTHEW   Baby Girl

PAULINE   JOSEPH

ALEX m. ANNIE

MARTIN m. COLETTA

BERNICE
LORETTA

STANCE

EMELINE m. FRANK
LILLA

BERNELL
HAROLD
RICHARD
MELVIN
DAVID
NANCY

SOPHIE m. ROMAN
DORAWA

IMELDA
SALLY ANN
ANTHONY
MABEL
SUZANNE

③ANNA ROSE
(AUNT ANNE)

JANE

MARY ELIZABETH m. ED
COLLARD

MIKE
DAVE
JOHN

VIRGINIA

① Anna of FIRST FARM IN THE VALLEY.

② Annie of WINDING VALLEY FARM.

③ Anna Rose of STAIRSTEP FARM.

④ Betsy of WILLOW WIND FARM.

⑤ Betsy of BETSY'S UP-AND-DOWN YEAR.

159